home
is not a
country

home
is not a
country

SAFIA ELHILLO

MAKE ME A WORLD

New York

MAKE ME A WORLD is an imprint dedicated to exploring the vast possibilities of contemporary childhood. We strive to imagine a universe in which no young person is invisible, in which no kid's story is erased, in which no glass ceiling presses down on the dreams of a child. Then we publish books for that world, where kids ask hard questions and we struggle with them together, where dreams stretch from eons ago into the future and we do our best to provide road maps to where these young folks want to be. We make books where the children of today can see themselves and each other. When presented with fences, with borders, with limits, with all the kinds of chains that hobble imaginations and hearts, we proudly say—no.

Text copyright © 2021 by Safia Elhillo
Jacket art copyright © 2021 by Shaylin Wallace, based on a photograph by Yael Marantz

All rights reserved. Published in the United States by Make Me a World, an imprint of Random House Children's Books, a division of Penguin Random House LLC, New York.

Make Me a World and the colophon are registered trademarks of Penguin Random House LLC.

Visit us on the Web! GetUnderlined.com

Educators and librarians, for a variety of teaching tools, visit us at RHTeachersLibrarians.com

Library of Congress Cataloging-in-Publication Data is available upon request.
ISBN 978-0-593-17705-1 (trade) — ISBN 978-0-593-17706-8 (lib. bdg.) — ISBN 978-0-593-17707-5 (ebook)

The text of this book is set in 11.5-point Adobe Caslon.
Interior design by Andrea Lau

Printed in the United States of America
March 2021
10 9 8 7 6 5 4 3 2 1

First Edition

To my communities. To Awrad & Basma.
You are my country.

Dear Reader,

The truth is, this is just one life of many you could have led.

At some point you made the choice to pick up this book, but you could have chosen something else to do. Before that there were other decisions—you chose to walk down one street or another, to take the bus, to talk to that stranger. Even earlier there were decisions made before you were born, decisions that have profoundly affected who you are right now, what language you speak, where you live, even how you dream.

It seems to me that this knowledge—that you could have just as easily been any one of a hundred other people—is at the heart of empathy. It's the realization that every person you meet, or see on the news, or hear about could have been you, if you had made slightly different choices, or if your grandparents had made different choices, going way back, into a great tree of different choices that looks like an entire world of people who aren't you, but might have been.

Some people have the gift of understanding that they could have been other people; Nima is one of them. She understands that her own life is just one branch of a tree, and the seeds that became her could have just as easily become someone else. She rides her nostalgia and the strange here-and-there-ness that is every immigrant's story to full visions of who she should have been if . . . And maybe we fantasize that we would be happier as that other person, or that we could run faster, or be more loved.

So many stories are about just this thing, the fantasy of what it would mean to be someone else. All the lions and wardrobes, all the kids with secret powers, even the cats in hats. But what they fail to realize is that just as much as there are the many people we could have been, these people live in the corners of imagination and, perhaps, they are wishing that they could be us.

Welcome, then, to Safia Elhillo's *Home Is Not a Country*, a tree of identities, of who we are and who we could be, and the dangerous and beautiful place in between.

Christopher Myers

MAKE ME A WORLD

PROLOGUE

NEW COUNTRY

The Photograph

in a lifetime before mine   my parents
not yet my parents   only a slim girl
the color of cinnamon   skirt swirled liquid
about her knees   as she dances   eyes cast
downward   smiling shyly at a boy
who mirrors her movement to the song   the little
gap in his front teeth   cigarette tucked
behind an ear   & shirt unbuttoned down his chest
sepia hand longing   for her waist   frozen
immortal in the photograph   wondering
if they will ever touch

Baba

the photographs of my father are everywhere

alone in a suit   framed in the living room

seated with his afro full
taped to the mirror of my mother's dresser

in the one on the coffee table he stares awestruck at his bride

a passport picture in mama's wallet
a single furrow in his brow

i like the ones of him younger   rounded & serious as a child

dusty-kneed as a teenager
crowded with other boys around a ball

before the car crash   that took him from knowing me

before the father-sized ache   before my mother all alone

still crowding herself to one side of the bed   saving his place

soft browns of the sepia photos
making him impossibly far away

Mama

in this photo   my mother is alone
as i will come to know her

it is her wedding day   back home
a lifetime right before mine   before
the new country   & the widowing
& the worry lines stamped into her brow

her eyelashes painted dark beneath
a headdress of silver coins
strung across her forehead
& her hands   floating up to fix
the arch of her headscarf
soil-colored blooms of henna
twisting from both elbows to
each finger

a different country   a different
life   the henna since faded
& the story hushed to memory
to old bits of song from oceans away

we are no longer back home
the headdress has been sold & my mother
is alone   is at work   is rushed
in her headscarf & blue jeans
& it hasn't been her wedding day in years

her name   aisha   means   *she who lives*
but mostly she goes to work & comes home tired
& watches television   & sometimes
in the television's blue glow
her eyes make tears that do not fall

i keep this photograph in a tin box
that once held butter biscuits
long ago eaten by guests   unimpressed
with our spare american living

Haitham

we've always known each other
our mothers friends from back home
bound into some ancient sisterhood
of grief   his mother the only one
who can make my mother laugh

but when i really meet him   when
we enter a siblinghood of our own
i am wearing the first new coat i have ever
owned & we are both entering the age that
makes our elbows feel larger than the rest
of our bodies

the wal-mart lights are cold & harsh
blunt squeak of his shoes against
the polished floors   nothing left of
my mother's date-palm trees   his
mother's riverbank   only suburban

america   no matter how far
we strain our eyes   our mothers
share a shopping cart & speak shy
quiet english   testing new words

like *coupon* & *value-pack*   his
polo shirt hangs loose about him
years before the shoulders
to come   & all they'll have to carry

later   at the bus stop   our mothers
fish for change at the bottoms
of their worn handbags   he lifts
the hem of his shirt   just a little
to show me a pack of stolen starburst
tucked into the waist of his jeans

are you going to tell?   he whispers
& i shake my head   thrumming
with excitement & fear   a grin
stretches across his face   *good*
he begins unwrapping the candy
because half of these are yours

School

i've never felt like i was good at anything
haitham   for all his atrocious grades
is at least good at people   while i am a solid
b minus in every class   & barely scraping
a passing grade in any social interaction
muttering & burdened by the shadow of an accent
that i cannot manage to make charming

at school haitham & i separate for the day
he's repeating ninth grade & we now have
different lunch periods   where i sit with
an assortment of others   all citizens of
the social margins   & though assembled
we do not talk   we poke glumly at our wilted lunches

i long ago begged mama to stop packing
leftovers for me to take to school   the smell alone
one morning   filled the entire bus despite
my seat in the back   where i waited
for everyone to pile out through the folding doors
before slumping outside myself   throwing away
the offending plastic container of okra & lamb & rice
before anyone could know it was mine

now instead i make my own dejected sandwiches
damp in their paper towels   two pieces of untoasted
white bread   & between them   a single slice
of plasticky american cheese

America

i go to halfhearted arabic classes each sunday
in a rented room at the middle school   &bleat
alef   baa   taa   thaa &agree with
haitham who sits behind me that this is   *like*
so boring

we never ask why our mothers had come here
& could not let it go   though i always beg
for the same crumpled photograph stories   of
weddings that went on for weeks   cafes crowded
with poets   gardens lush & humming
with mosquitoes

we whisper to each other   *if it's so great there*
then why don't we ever go back

but i have always listened to the stories
& every day   i long   at school i still
do not speak   i wear the same
fleece sweatshirt   washed & rewashed

the girl who sits behind me in math
came over once to work
on a project   told everyone after
that it smelled   *like rice & dirty plants*
wondered aloud if my mother
was bald under the headscarf

in my silence i dress myself
in yellow & imagine
a garden thick with date palms

a girl   mouth open & fluent
who knows where she is from

Yasmeen

my mother meant to name me   for her favorite flower
its sweetness   garlands made   for pretty girls
for parties   to be worn thick in heavy hair

instead i got this name   & i don't even know why
maybe named for some unknown dead relative
some dreary ghost   so of course   no one wants me
at their party   their sleepover   their after-school
trip to the mall

of course i fade   to the back of the classroom   the photos
& in the hallways no one looks my way
some days i walk to school because the bus driver
does not see me at the stop
& when i spot my homeroom teacher   in the supermarket
she glances & squints like she isn't quite sure who i am

i imagine her   yasmeen   this other girl   bright & alive
mouth full & dripping with language   easy in her charm
& in essence she looks like me   but of course
better   nails unbitten & painted turquoise   her hair
unknotted & long   ears glittering with stud earrings
not like mine   thick with keloid from an infected piercing

i imagine her back home   fathered   beloved
knowing all the songs & all their corresponding dances
laughing big & showing all her teeth
invited to all the parties

called to from across the street by classmates   by teachers
jewel of the neighborhood & somehow
a little taller than me
like there are extra bones in her spine
like everyone knows her name   & i ache
to have been born her   instead

Nostalgia Monster

haitham calls me a *nostalgia monster*   & likes to laugh
at the dream-brain that takes over mine when i hear
the old songs   & run my fingers
over the old photographs   i know the words
to the old films   & imagine myself gliding in
to join the dance   glamorous in black & white
photographed in sepia   frozen in a perfect time

i wish our arabic teacher would tell us more
about what it was like back then   before everyone
left   when they were young & dreaming
& hearing the songs crackling out of a radio
but i cannot imagine him young or dancing
cannot imagine him any way except the way we know
him now   scowling over conjugations & how
we mispronounce the language   how it wilts
on our american tongues

one of my favorites is a sayed khalifa song
where he sings to a girl he calls a pearl necklace
يا عقد اللولي   لولي
يا بنت يا حلوة يا لولي

& says   وين الحلوين وين راحوا
where are the beautiful ones   where did they go
& i think he means us   all the ones who left
all the gone

My Name

nima   well really it's نِعمة   *ni'ma*
mispronounced at school to sound like
the middle of the word *animal*   or stretched
into a whining   *neema*   no letter in english
for the snarling sound that centers my name
its little growl   ع

nima   meaning *grace*   it would be funny
if it weren't cruel   i stumble over my own overlarge
feet   & knock over the clay incense holder   its coal
burning a perfect circle into the wooden table   i brush
an uncoordinated elbow past the counter & the tray
holding tea for guests   a full set of dishes
teapot & milk jug & sugar bowl & saucers
& matching cups   painted
with tiny flowers   goes crashing to the tiled floor
i trip on the carpet's hem & fall   chipping a tiny corner
of my bottom front tooth   & in calling my name
in exasperation my mother   calls
for the grace i don't have

PART 1

THE OTHER SIDE

The Airport

once when i was small   we packed a shared suitcase
of bright cotton   floral prints   & something yellow
& silken i'd never seen my mother wear
& for the trip across the country she wore perfume
& her best red beaded scarf   & we clattered
into the terminal   my mother   collecting all the light

a wedding on another coast   its promises
of sunlight & gold   & her scattered schoolmates
& cousins & faraway friends   all crowded
into a rented hall   making it   with color
& incense & song   our country
& it all shone in my mother's face

we approached the counter to check in   the family
ahead of ours handed their boarding passes with a grin
before the agent turned to us & his smile clicked shut
said   *check-in is closed*   & no
there is nothing he can do
& no there is no manager to call & please can we leave
this counter is now closed

my mother's faltering voice   the soft music in her english
her welling eyes   her wilting face   her beaded scarf
& all she said was *please*   *please*   *i have a ticket*
& i'd never seen her so small   english fleeing her mouth
& leaving her faltering   frozen   reaching for words
that would not come   dabbing at her eyes

with the scarf   its red so bright   so festive
like it was mocking us

& all i could do was reach   for the suitcase with one hand
her limp arm with the other   & wheel us to the exit
& in our slow retreat i heard the last snatches
of that man's joke   his colleague's barking laugh
no way we're letting
mohammed so-and-so near the plane
& that's why we don't go anywhere   anymore

Mama

my mother is so often sad   so often tired & wants mostly
to sit quietly in front of the television   where we watch
turkish soap operas dubbed over in arabic
their sweeping landscapes & enormous romances
until she falls asleep
chin pointed into her chest & glasses askew

on bright days she plays music   pitches her voice high
& sings along to all the ones we love   abdel halim
& wardi & fairouz   sayed khalifa & oum kalthoum
gisma's open throaty voice & frantic percussion
to which mama claps along   tries sometimes to teach me
the dances   the body formed like a pigeon's
the chest arced proudly upward   head twisting helixes
against the neck   in a surprise to no one i cannot dance
but love to watch her   love that she tries anyway
to teach me

& sometimes   rarely   by some magic   the movement
will click fluently into my body   & she'll ululate & clap
while i twist my head in time to the song   mama's voice
celebratory & trilling   *my nima   my graceful girl*

Haitham

is smaller than me   three weeks younger & always
a little disheveled   always dressed in something that
someone else wore first   & laughs
the most enormous sound

haitham passes me a drawing   during arabic class
full-color cartoon on the back of a worksheet
of our horrible teacher   spit flying from his
large mouth   with a speech bubble that reads
*WE ARE NOT AMERRICANS! YOU SPEAK
ZE ARRABIC!*   eyes bulging & his bald patch
glistening in the light

i press my fist over my mouth to keep the laugh inside
& it builds until i think my eyeballs might burst
until the sound threatens to come pouring from my
ears   from my nose   until my face is wet
with tears

& haitham swipes the drawing   crumples it
into his notebook   right as the teacher turns
& thunders over   spits a little while asking
what *on earth*   (the only way teachers are allowed
to say *the hell*)   what on earth is wrong with me
i only manage to choke out   *allergies*
& haitham   from the row behind   offers me
a tissue with a grin

Pyramids

once   in arabic class   excited that the new girl's name
luul   reminded me of the song i love   the pearl necklace

i sang a little of it when she introduced herself
& watched her smile falter   confused   before she finally

excused herself   & by the end of the day everyone
was giggling   *nima loves old people's music   pass it on*

so even here among my so-called people i do not fit
here where the hierarchy puts those who have successfully

americanized   at the top   i've marked myself by caring
about the old world   & now i hover somewhere

at the bottom of the pyramid   (while our arabic teacher
drones about ancient times   & the little-known fact

that *our country has 255 pyramids remaining today*)
the bottom of the pyramid with those recently arrived

dusty-shoed & heavy-tongued   & though i'm born here
though my love of the old songs & old photos

doesn't translate to my spelling   my handwriting
my arabic pronunciation   or grammar   or history

or memorization of the qur'an   i recognize
in their widened eyes   that feeling   that shock

of being here instead of there

Haitham

lives in my building   which isn't actually surprising
since it seems everyone from our country immigrated
to this same block of crowded apartments

it's saturday morning & he's ringing the doorbell
frantic   & falls inside when i answer
sweaty & rumpled & still in his house shoes   coughing
with a little joke in his eye

his grandmother   opening his t-shirt drawer   to put away
the laundry   found his secret pack of cigarettes   which
he doesn't even really smoke   which he tried to explain
away   while dodging the slippers aimed at his head
who knew mama fatheya was so athletic
everything always so funny to him
she chased him out with cries of
DISKUSTING!   DISKUSTING!   & where else
was he going to go

my mother hasn't left yet for work   & makes us tea
boiled in milk   poured into mismatched mugs
& hands us packs of captain majid cookies she gets
from the bigala that haitham & i call   ethnic wal-mart
where we buy everything   from bleeding legs of lamb
to patterned pillow covers   & cassettes
covered in a layer of dust

she never seems old enough to be anyone's mother
so pretty & unlined & smelling always of flowers

she clears the cups & wipes the crumbs from the table
& our faces in quick movements   pins her scarf
around her face & leaves for work

haitham isn't wearing shoes so we cannot go outside
we instead spend the day playing our favorite game
calling all our people's typical names out the window
into the courtyard   *mohammed!   fatimah!   ali!   bedour!*
to see how many strangers startle   & look up
when they are called

Haitham

haitham's grandmother once asked us   suspicious
what do you two do all day?   & by the middle of the list
had already turned her eyes back to the television
as haitham continued to list our every microscopic act
music videos   *snacks*   *monopoly*
even though half the cards are missing   *five-dollar tuesdays*
at the movie theater after school
concan even though nima thinks i cheat
& we don't really know the rules
& in truth i do not know what we really do
with our time together
because it's always been like this
my every day is filled with haitham
his laughter pulling my own to join it
our nonsense jokes & riffs
& misremembered lyrics & laughing & more laughing
i see him every day & somehow still have so much to tell him
every time one of us rings the doorbell to the other's apartment
& crosses the threshold   already beginning whatever story
already unfolding whatever thought   & he's never
joined the other kids in making fun
of all my strangeness   makes it feel instead
like a good thing
even when he calls me *the nostalgia monster*
he makes it sound like a compliment
full of affection & pure joy   has never
made me feel that there is anything wrong with me at all

An Illness

through the bathroom door i hear haitham singing loudly
in the shower   stretching each note with a flourish

i perch next to mama fatheya on the couch
while she watches   intent

as a woman on the television pulls a glistening chicken
from the oven   i am so bored   & haitham

is taking his time   the mantel above the television
is crowded with photographs

haitham's mother   khaltu hala   younger & first arrived
her hair cut short & eyes haunted

haitham a bundle in her arms   *mama fatheya,*
tell me about back home   she glances up from

her program   irritated at first & then softening
nostalgia is an illness, little one   she says gently

turning back to the television   but continues
ours is a culture that worships yesterday over tomorrow

but i think we are all lucky to have left yesterday
behind   we are here now

dissatisfied   i press on   *wait, you actually*
like it here?   & she faces me again   a sadness hitched

behind her eyes   *here i have lost nothing i could not*
afford to lose

just as haitham squawks the last notes to his song
& shuts off the shower   i look at the lost country

in mama fatheya's face   & recognize it
from my own mother's face   the face of every grown-up

in our community   a country i've never seen
outside a photograph

& i miss it too

Haitham

always laughing & pulling laughter from anyone he meets
has interests that keep him here instead of dreaming
of a lost world   for a while he tried to get me
to play video games   but i could not make myself care
& now i mostly sit on the plastic-covered couch
& watch him play while i daydream   & when he's done
or tired of losing   he'll put on one of the old movies
from the box under his grandmother's bed   though by now
we've watched them all dozens of times   we each
pick a favorite character & recite all the dialogue
long since memorized   & squawk off-key
to all the songs   though secretly we are each belting
them out in earnest

i think that   secretly   he loves
this old world almost as much as i do

Khaltu Hala

haitham's mother   her hair cut close around her ears
though in the old pictures she wore it long   puffed out
around her shoulders   curls halfway down her back

i like her   her gruffness & briskness & her short bark
of a laugh   the books shelved floor to ceiling
in the little apartment   each one of them hers
traced for years by her fingers until the ink
began to gray   the way she coaxes a smile
from my mother   & clears the shadow from her face
the way she growls out every letter of my name
in approval   how i can't imagine her ever afraid
though when she is home we don't watch the old films
or sing the old songs or ask too many questions

my mother never talks about it except the one time
after khaltu hala heard me humming the song
about the pearl necklace   &   eyes bulging
voice hoarse   told me to leave   & go home
knocking gently on our door hours later
a little pearl ring passed from her hand to mine
her embrace bright with the smell of oranges & soap
apology muffled by my sweatshirt's thick fabric

that night   my mother   voice hushed   told me
about the officers that cut khaltu hala's hair   the long scars
striped down her back   the thousand things
she will not talk about   in hopes of erasing
that whole country   & starting again here

brand-new   & i almost wish she hadn't told me
& for weeks after i did not want to listen
to the songs   & every photograph looked sharper & ugly
& gave off the faintest smell of copper   of blood
& now i mostly try to forget the story   & return to loving
the dream of home   & the pearl never leaves my finger

Mama

though the story about khaltu hala hurts   i do not
want my mother to stop telling stories   she who

so rarely tells anything at all   i ask
about my grandmother   *loved flowers*   about

my mother as a young girl   *i wanted to be*
a dancer   & when i ask about my name

she frowns a little   squinting as she chooses
the words   *i had a whole other name picked out,*

did you know?   *but when your father died*
i don't know   *it felt like that name belonged to him*

& i couldn't bear to keep it without him   *so i picked*
something else   & i feel that old pang   of being

second-best   to that other girl   my ghost-self
                                yasmeen

Overheard

my mother has guests over & i am hiding in my room
humming to myself & looking through my tin box
of artifacts   the photographs again   my mother as
a painted bride   my parents dancing   i put the pictures
away   the cassettes   & hear my mother calling me
to greet her guests   *hello   fine thank you*
i'm almost fifteen   school's fine
arabic's fine   alhamdulillah   you too
& i duck back into hiding

& i hear khaltu amal with the tattooed eyebrows
who is not actually my aunt & who always smells like ghee
purring to my mother   *she could be such a pretty girl*
& my mother mourning my unkemptness   *sometimes*
she won't even brush her hair   & i don't know why
she insists on wearing that sweatshirt all the time
i have to pry it away to wash   & khaltu amal again
her cloying voice   *remember when we were girls?*
the daughters we imagined we'd have?   & i hate her
& her pink-gray face   her still-brown neck she hasn't
bothered to bleach to match   i hate her armful
of clattering bangles   the way she touches my mother's
arm & pretends to be her friend   the way she wrinkles
her nose whenever she enters our apartment   her own
apartment large & expensive but filled with awful gaudy
objects   i giggle a little to myself at the memory of haitham
saying to her   straight-faced
aunt amal, would you agree that money can't buy
taste?   though my laugh dies as i hear her continue

to mama   *remember the girl you wanted to name*
yasmeen?   with yellow ribbons braided into her hair
such a pretty name   i never understood
why you chose the other

& in the mirror i try to unknot the hair tangled at my neck
& of course there's no point   i give up & stare
into my blurring reflection   my body filled
with strange static   & see only a smudge where my nose
& mouth should be   only the eyes
large & blinking & intact   & when i blink again it's back
the same unremarkable face

Mama

of course i know my mother is lonely
her days & nights spent mostly in the company
of ghosts   so much of who & what she's loved
she speaks of only in past tense   though mostly
she keeps quiet   i can't help but imagine
that her life was enormous before we came here
loud & crowded & lively as any party
& then the final notes of the song   & everyone
is gone   except me   & i feel my own smallness
as i try to fill her life's empty spaces
though they gape around me like the one pair
of her high-heeled shoes i used to love
to play with when i was little   so much of our life
feels like sitting at a table set for dozens
who will never again arrive   the two of us surrounded
by empty chairs   my mother is lonely
& i am her daughter   her only   i think that might be why
i'm lonely too

The Photographs

the photographs are how i piece together
my imagining of my mother's first life
when she was aisha   life of the party
a girl in a yellow dress who was going
to be a dancer   loved & laughing
& never lonely   a whole life stretched
before her in the company of friends
& family & the man she chose
who chooses her & knows all
her favorite songs   who watches her
with awe   & never dies   his life
braided tightly to the long bright ribbon of hers

i don't think she even knows i have them
these pictures   i've had them for years
in the box i keep under my bed
& she's never noticed   because she never
asks for them   because she hasn't looked
at them in years

Mama

when i was little i always tried to make her smile

it's why i learned the songs   why i learned all

their words   why i learned to love them

the smiles were always rare   though lately they feel

even rarer   & in their absence i keep myself company

with the songs she taught me to love   the dream

of a lost world where she was happiest

i miss him too   my father   though we never met

i miss the country that i've never seen   the cousins

& aunts & grandparents   i miss the help

they could have offered   the secrets they knew

that i never learned   of how to keep her smiling

Overheard

it's saturday & i wake messily   sweating & crumpled
& somehow sure that it's closer to afternoon than morning

through my closed door i can hear mama & khaltu hala
their easy chatter a low hum   the clinking of sugar

being stirred into coffee   something meaty & unfamiliar
wafting its smells from the stove   when i move to investigate

i hear a shriek   & rush to open the door   see my mother
doubled over in her seat   her shoulders shaking

& for a sinking   sickening moment   i'm sure she's crying
i turn to look at khaltu hala to find out what happened

but she's smiling   shaking her head as mama rises
face shining with the tears i'd suspected

but she's laughing

trying & failing to catch her breath before another peal escapes
khaltu hala catches my eye   motions to the kitchen

i made turkey chili   *go make yourself a plate*   i point my chin
quizzically at mama   my eyes on khaltu hala for an answer

& she chuckles   *your mother is making fun of my fine*
american cooking   *she keeps calling the chili* دمعة خواجات

white people curry   & another peal rings out from mama
alongside khaltu hala's hoot of laughter

my own fit of giggles joining them

Another Life

in the dream i am back home & i am beautiful   my country
wrapped like an embrace around me   my god not hated
my language washed of all its hesitation   my father
alive   alive   he never gets into the car that night
(my mother will not talk about it except to say
there was a car   an accident)   in the dream
he never gets into the car   stays home instead reading
poems aloud to my mother   rubbing almond oil into
her already-soft feet   sitting for hours on the front steps
of their house   pointing to the moon's perfect reflection
in the river below   in the dream he stays alive   stays
alive   alive   stays alive to meet me

Baba

i think   if he'd lived   my father would have been
a famous singer   crooning & preening in a shiny suit
his hair dense & dark   or maybe   an artist
throwing clay onto a potter's wheel & shaping creatures
from its mass like some sort of smaller god   or maybe
an athlete   muscle & vein cording in his still-strong legs
a scientist serious in goggles & white   a writer pulling
stacks of books from his knotted brain   a television star
his face so familiar he's almost everyone's father   but
always mostly mine   coming home in the evenings
to swing me up onto his back & run circles until i'm dizzy
holding my hand in his callused grasp   teaching me
the songs he loved   the songs he danced to
with my mother   unwidowed & smiling with all
her teeth   twirled in the living room
dress billowing over her calves   loved   both of us
belonging to someone   tied together by the belonging
by my father   my father   no longer gone

Haitham

tonight haitham does the funniest impression
of abdel halim hafez   pitches his voice as deep
as it will go & croons all my favorite songs
on tape so beautiful that they make me want to cry
but when he does them   i can't choke back the laugh
i join him in my own awful singing voice
نار يا حبيبي نار   اه يا حبيبي بحبك

& his grandmother is so superstitious but also maybe
just irritated by our squawking voices drowning out
her television program   tells us not to be so rowdy
at twilight because that is when the fine skin between
our world & the next is thinnest

don't run after sundown because the jinn will trip you
don't raise your voice or you will call them to our side
& i'm supposed to be too old to be scared by these things
but it works   & when haitham opens his mouth
to sing again i suggest we watch a movie instead

Boys

simply put   haitham has other friends
though outside of school   back in our building
his time is mostly mine   always home when i knock
always knocking when i'm home

but at school   where we have no classes together
& different lunch periods   i see him sometimes
in the hallway   where he will always smile or wave
then return to startling laughter from the mouths
of his friends   that tangle of big-shouldered boys
their smell of musk & salt   crowded around haitham's
smaller frame   though among them he seems not only
to fit in   but taller   their crown jewel
their beating heart

for a while he tried to invite me places with them
movies & parties & diners & the arcade   & i've never
said yes   always too shy & feeling increasingly
hot & confused by their boy-smell   their big teeth & hands
the ways i sometimes want both to be looked at
& to disappear

i think always of the version of myself i'd want them to see
to look at in awe   to never look away   that better
& beautiful version of me   that version named yasmeen
deserving of each & every pair of their eyes   but as myself
i am mostly happy to wave back to haitham in the hallway
& sneak a glance at the backs   of the other boys' unturned
heads

The Mirror

some nights   when mama is working late
& haitham is with his other friends
i sit at mama's dresser   its enormous mirror
stretched before me   mama's rarely used jars
& powders   darkening my lashes   flushing
my cheeks   carving cheekbones into the roundness
of my features   a yellow dress from its hanger
wedged in the back of mama's closet   its bright silk
from a forgotten time

& in the mirror i become another girl   i become yasmeen
i practice smiling & laughing & imagine myself
talking to the boys   i imagine that i am beautiful
i imagine someone is looking   i play as if
for an audience   i coach a twang into my voice
& twirl a lock of hair around my finger

tonight the hair catches in khaltu hala's ring
& i barely have enough time to untangle it
& slip mama's dress back into the closet
i hurry into the bathroom as she arrives

Videos

what i'll never share with anyone is my true
guilty pleasure   every weekday after school
the hour or so before haitham comes knocking on my door
when my mother is still hours away from returning home
i'll push the coffee table off to the side   & watch
american music videos   try to shape my limbs & waist
to match their dancers   their high-heeled singers
& imagine my body as one of theirs instead
& i always feel a little less lonely
loving these songs that everyone loves too

but tonight   with the volume turned high
i do not hear my mother's key in the door
& she walks in to find me trying awkwardly
to keep pace with a dance   missing the beat
& then catching it only to miss it once again
& when i turn to see her standing   smiling
watching me   the shame courses hot
through my now-frozen limbs   & i am so
embarrassed i start to cry   i scramble
for my room   & will not emerge for dinner
avoid her eyes for days until i'm sure
she will not mention it

English

most of the other kids in my arabic class
learned english like haitham did   by talking
to people   speaking up in school   going
to movies with classmates   being invited
to sleepovers   to parties

when haitham & i were younger we would mostly
speak to each other in arabic   until one day
when he announced   that if we were ever going
to lose our accents   we would have to speak
english with each other   though these days
we kind of have our own language
a perfect mix of the two   so we never have
to translate   & the words can come out
in whichever language we think them in

i didn't learn the way he did   by talking
to anyone else   by making any other friends
i learned alone   at home with the television
with the radio   learning those songs too
not just the ones from back home   i knew all
the ones from here too   sang them softly
to myself in my room   in the shower
training out my accent   shaping my mouth
around the twang   sparkling & new

English

standing at my locker   i stuff books & papers
into my backpack to go home   laughter & chatter
buzzing all around me   i imagine myself
as its silent center   a black hole in the universe

a big group of boys & girls are clattering together
down the hallway   joking & squealing
as one of the boys reaches to tickle a girl
her giggles & shrieks piercing the entire hallway
before she breaks off into a run to escape
& he follows   knocking into me & sending
my backpack flying   loose papers & books
& pencils scattering everywhere

they both briefly look back   & he calls out
sorry!   & over the noise of the group returning
to its chatter   i hear the girl say   as i bend
to crush everything back into my bag   *i don't think
she speaks english*

Halloween

haitham rides with me to school & today walks
with me to my locker   joking about the costumes we pass
who's going to tell jason that dumb jock isn't a costume
do you think tara knows that costume is racist

& we pass a tall boy dressed like a ghost from one of those
old movies   just a sheet with two eyeholes cut out
& i say to haitham   thinking no one else will hear
how original   & the boy behind the sheet turns
to me   making sure his friends are within earshot
calls in his voice muffled by fabric

i'm dressed as your terrorist mom   & everyone
howls with laughter   another wraps a sweater
around his head like a turban   *& i'm*
your terrorist dad   & haitham steps in front
don't say that   her father's dead   but his small voice
drowns in all the chaos

i look down & watch my feet flicker in & out of their outline
my body humming with shame   i am a ghost
from no movie anyone would care enough to make

the boys have already forgotten us
& moved farther down the hall
my eyes feel hot & i hate that i'm going to cry

Mama

when i was little i loved to wrap myself
in my mother's scarves   what felt like
a thousand colors   knotted into gowns
into headbands   covering my sleeping body
on the couch halfway through a movie

what i loved most was to drape one
after another over my face   breathe in
her smell of sandalwood & flowers   & look out
into the world in its new colors   the sky
made purple by the pink chiffon   made green
by the yellow one   the whole apartment
becoming a painting

after that day at the airport years ago
i thought she'd stop wearing it   & once
asked her why she didn't   & she lifted
for a moment from her crumpled sadness
into something harder   *nima, i need you*
to understand that it was those men
who were wrong   not us   i will never
be ashamed of where i come from
i will never let you be ashamed
of who we are   & what i didn't ask
is what made her so sure

Yasmeen

it's twilight   i'm home alone & singing
along to my cassettes in my loudest voice
& already feeling a little better
twirling about like in the old movies
where everyone sings & somehow
knows all the words   نار يا حبيبي نار

& maybe i'm too old to be afraid
of being left in the apartment by myself
but i keep thinking i see movement in the corner
of my eye   snap my head around to find nothing

& to prove to myself that i am brave i close
my eyes   throw my head back & sing
even louder   اه يا حبيبي بحبك
& when i open my eyes she is standing
in the corner of the room

& she looks like me   but overall somehow better
longer in the spine   hair smooth & nails unbitten
& so solid i know she's there   but with something
blurred around her edges   & when she opens
her mouth she speaks in my voice except
she speaks in perfect arabic   & her very first word
is my name

nima   graceful one   don't you wonder
don't you wonder
don't you   & the air behind her shimmers

like interrupted water   figures swimming through it
like fish   my father's face   muscled & moving
a skyline   two rivers & a date palm
a doum tree   an old woman in a yellow tobe
her face just like my mother's   & yet another me
holding court to a cluster of cinnamon-colored girls
our arms around each other's waists   & all of it could be
real enough to touch if i wasn't too scared to move

i retreat into my head   & remember mama fatheya's
warnings about the spirit world at twilight   stories
of children trapped on the other side   but the girl
before me can't be a jinni   she's me   maybe she's
my sister   a twin i never knew   a secret   she's real
enough to touch & doesn't seem at all evil
but i'm scared   & she's so blurred around the edges
like a reflection in water   my mother would not like this
& would tell me to recite my prayers   to protect myself
from jinn   protect myself from their temptations
i'm not sure this is what she meant but just in case
i look squarely at the girl who i know now is yasmeen
my other me   & tell her to leave me alone

Yasmeen

my mother is watching television   one of those
egyptian soap operas crowded with big-bodied

fast-talking light-skinned women   wailing
& slapping their cheeks   i can't follow the story & feel

how clumsy my arabic is   i start & falter & start again
mama   & she is too absorbed in the program to hear me

mama, something happened   she lowers
the volume & turns to me   & looks so tired

i think it might be wrong to burden her   & what even
do i have to say   *why did you name me nima?*

speak arabic   why did you give me this name?
what happened?   her attention is slipping away

& a mustached character on the television just slapped
another character   who i think is supposed to be his brother

mama   silence   mama   what is it?   an edge
of irritation in her voice & i know i cannot tell her

about last night & make it make sense   but she is looking
at me now   a single worry line in her perfect face

& all i want is her protection   her attention   i want her to
pull me in & tell me not to be afraid   to stroke my head

& murmur a prayer into the part in my hair   i don't know
how to make her believe me   about the girl i saw

yasmeen   i don't know that i believe it
myself   *what is it, habiba?*   & i know

i can't tell her   so instead i say   *a boy at school
called me a terrorist*

& the ready tear in her eye starts to fall

Haitham

meets me at the park   & climbs onto the swing
next to mine   already telling some story   some
joke   *haitham*   he doesn't hear me   *haitham*
what?   & i don't know what to say first   to tell him
about yasmeen   or that i'm mad at him for telling
those boys about my dad   but all i can muster is
do you believe in jinn?   *what?*
you know, all those stories your grandmother tells
she just makes those up to scare us
but what if they're true?

he raises an eyebrow & breaks into a grin   *you know,*
nima, you're lucky i'm the only one who knows
how weird you are   which would normally make me laugh
but today it cuts   today it sounds like *you don't have*
any other friends   i am full of hurt   full of anger
& i just need somewhere to put it   i am so sick of carrying
it around   so i let myself give in
i let it take over my voice   i let it take over my entire
body   *how could you just tell everyone about*
my dad like that? it's so easy for you to tell my business,
but where's your dad? why don't you tell that story instead?
or actually   i feel intoxicated   possessed   i lick my lips
& continue   *why don't you just leave me alone?*
you know the only reason we're even friends is because
you live down the hall   we're not even in the same grade
anymore   why don't you go bother
some other ninth grader   & i storm away   the swings
creaking on their chains behind me

Bathwater

later   in the bathtub i replay it all behind my eyes
embarrassed by my overreaction   missing haitham
already   too frozen by shame to apologize

i look down at my hands warping underwater   he's right
there's something weird about me   my body filled
with an unfamiliar current   my hands flitting in
& out of focus   even when i blink & look again
i lift the left one out of the bathwater to study in the light
translucent as my mother's best chiffon   i try to touch
the bathtub & both hands pass through the ceramic
& my body goes hot again   this time with fear
my hands flicker a final time
then go solid   i give them one last shake
& scramble   slippery   out of the bath

Haitham

i see him at school & he will not look at me
i keep checking my hands   sure that i have
once again   gone invisible   but they're there

every day he's surrounded by others
making jokes & laughing his enormous laugh   & i won't
be the first to apologize   the shame still warm
in my stomach   but without him i sometimes go days
without speaking out loud
my mother at work & then tired
my cassettes wounding me with their familiar songs

i go home & climb into bed before it gets dark
& still feel heavy & tired in the morning
today i fall asleep again in math   & when i wake
i can see the desk
through the hum of my translucent arm

Advice

my head is in my mother's lap   her cool hands
on my cheek & in my hair   & for a long time
she's quiet   unbothered by the tears & snot
soaking into her skirt

at your age   she finally says   *you shouldn't be spending*
so much time with boys   *why don't you talk to some*
of the girls in your arabic class   & she stops when i start
crying so hard my skull feels too tight for my brain

& we sit like this for what feels eternal   she sighs
& smooths my hair   *i see you two together & it doesn't*
seem right for you to be apart   *i'm sure he misses*
you too   *why don't you try giving him a call*

Calling Haitham

his grandmother answers the phone & though it's late
she tells me haitham isn't home   she sounds surprised
he told me he was with you   i feel a little prickle
of guilt   knowing he's going to be in trouble
& it seems rude   just hanging up the call without asking
after mama fatheya's health   so i chew my thumbnail
while she lists the day's creaking & aches

i study my hands for another nail to bite   & remember
them shimmering in the bathwater   though today
they are solid & warm with blood   & when she finally
pauses for breath i see my chance   *mama fatheya,*
what do you know about jinn? are they real? are they bad?
do they really ever come to our side?

i hear her groan into her chair with a sigh
& wet her lips before she begins
of course they're real   *there are all sorts of creatures*
you know   *nearly human & just outside our line of sight*
they've never given me any trouble   *though of course*
i use the stories to get you children to behave
my husband   *(god rest his soul) couldn't see them & just*
thought the house was haunted   *they rarely*
linger   *& on this side they don't look fully there*

& of course you must have heard   *there was*
a nasty rumor for some time   *right after you were*
born   *that there were two of you in the womb*

the other girl never born   *one child for each parent*
one child for each world   i hear her bite wetly
into something & chew while she thinks   *anyway*
why do you ask

Jinn

maybe yasmeen was sent to bring me home
to my father   his other daughter
my other me   maybe i am fading from this world
to grow solid on the other side

Boys

i pass haitham & his friends in the hall
& without his usual wave & smile he becomes
another brick in the impenetrable wall of boys
who don't see me

again today they laugh & run & shove
their way down the hallway   & again
as i stand at my locker   my open backpack
is knocked over by one of their games
this time two of haitham's friends   this time
no one apologizes   i look up from
my scattered books to find haitham
walking away with them
haitham   impossibly far away
haitham who will not turn to look at me

Arabic Class

haitham still sits behind me in arabic class on sunday
though when i arrive he is already showing something
in his notebook   to a girl sitting next to him
& they laugh together & do not stop
or look up as i take my seat

as the teacher drones on i study each face around
the classroom   the popular ones i secretly think of
as the americans   spotless high-top sneakers
the girls in zigzagged braids & tight t-shirts   the boys
with the slightly swollen piercing in their left ears
where they'd been forced to remove the earring
before coming to class

the girl talking to haitham is wearing jeans that look
brand-new   the baby hairs at her hairline slicked
down with a toothbrush   & through her eyes
i try to see his scrawniness   his used-up clothes
& instead find only the face carved from marble
geometry of the cheekbones   little gap in his teeth
as he laughs his way through another joke
new broadness of his shoulders
that makes him look   despite his short stature
like he takes up all the space in the room

i remember when we first started coming here
when i'd just started growing & all my clothes
were too small   overhearing some girl whisper
to another   that i wore such tight jeans

because i didn't have a father   & before
i could even think to cry   haitham leaning up
from his seat behind me   to ponder loudly
that if both her parents had let her out of the house
with that ugly t-shirt on   then i was honestly
better off with just the one   i remember
being warmed by the ring of my own laugh
& feel myself sitting alone now   haunted
by that old & forgotten sound

The Headscarf

i know something happened on the news again
because my mother has stopped wearing her scarf
to work   & instead tucks each strand of her hair
into a knit hat   the nape of her neck new
& tender in the light   she who once said
i will never be ashamed of where i come from
i will never let you be ashamed of who we are
seems to have changed her mind   & i wonder
if this means i should feel ashamed too

i float through another day at school
sleeping & flickering & talking to no one
so many times each day i look down to see
my arms   legs   stomach gone translucent
& each time i think   with something almost
like relief   that i will finally disappear   my body
returns   & i think i've made the whole thing up

at day's end i clang my locker shut
& four boys   large enough to block out the light
are closing in around me

one pulls the neck of his t-shirt up around his face
a clumsy hijab   two others hoot with laughter
& follow suit   & for a moment i think they might
forget me   laughing together & enjoying their joke
a strip of pale midriff showing on each torso
one of them is silent then cuts in   *my dad's a pilot*
his voice wet with poison   *he could have been*

on that plane   i think he might cry & the sound
he chokes out   makes the hair on the back of my neck
prickle up   he turns & shoves me
& i feel the cold metal of the lockers against my back
terrorist bitch   he spits into my hair

i raise my arms to cover my face   i cower & still
they move in closer   my blood feels hot
& swirls messily through my body
i press my eyes shut & will myself to vanish
but when they open i am still there
dampening with sweat   i cry out for yasmeen
& they hesitate   when nothing happens the boy's hand
clamps onto my shoulder   & wrenches me to the ground
i hear my heartbeat roaring in my ears

he snarls in pain   i look up
& i am outside the circle   standing upright & opaque
blood packed underneath my nails

The Office

i didn't get to wash my hands & that's proof enough
that i started it   he's bleeding & i am not

though given their number   & how they tower over me
the principal decides   it wasn't one-sided

& therefore   it's only fair   to suspend all five of us
& sends us out while he calls our homes   one by one

Outside the Office

my mother is at work   & i'm not allowed to leave
until someone comes for me   my nails are bitten
to the quick & sting   i can't scrape out
the dark lines of blood

one by one   the other mothers file in   painted
& hairsprayed & perfumed   clicking in their heeled
shoes & bustling into the principal's office
without looking at me   not even bothering
to shut the door

their indignation rings out into the hall
no way would my son   varsity   honor roll
his permanent record   my son   my son
an emotional time   you know, of course,
that his father's a pilot?   says she screamed at them
in her language   menacing   so of course, you understand
you understand   thank you   exactly
i knew you'd understand   & he walks them out
to their cars   where they shake hands   all smiling

Why Here

around sunset   mama fatheya comes to get me
i tell the office she is my grandmother
& does not speak any english   they look into
her wizened face & find its matching brown
in mine   & let her take me home

my shirt is torn & when she asks all i'll say
is that i fought another girl   i tell her my mother
will be home soon   thank her & let myself
into the apartment   where i sit for hours
on our noisy couch   still covered in its plastic

i am too tired to move   to wash or change
my ripped clothes   or scrub my fingernails
with a brush until the blood is my own

dusk falls & night falls further   my mother's key
clicks into the door   & she walks in to find me
silent in the dark   shirt torn & something
breaking behind my eyes   & before she can ask
i am frothing with anger   at everything   at her

the name tag crooked on her ill-fitting blouse
the hat slipping from her face & showing strands
of her still-dark hair   her sad too-blue jeans
my only family   my only person   & it all
feels like her fault   *why did you bring us here?*
they hate us   silence   she does not tell me
to speak arabic   *why did you bring me here*

to be tortured   to be alone   why would you
do that to me?   she opens her mouth to speak
& nothing comes out   my anger grows a second
head   & makes me cruel   *i wish baba was here*
instead of you   i wish someone was here who
could protect me   & i will not stay to see her cry
so i shuffle into the bathroom
to run the water to scalding

Ghosts

after i've sat in the bath until the water
gets cold   i climb out & dry off
walk out to see my mother sitting
dejected   on the couch   her face
in her tired hands

before i can slink off to my room
i hear her voice   a new sharpness
nima   come here   tell me
what happened   & for a moment
i think of telling her everything
instead of carrying it all around
myself   i think of laying my head
in her lap & asking her to help
to carry some of it with me

but at the sight of her head covered
in that sad knit hat   i know
i will not give her anything more
to carry   i can't   so all i say
is that i fought another girl
at school   & i am almost relieved
by her anger   the way it hardens
her soft & hurt places   *i don't even*
know who you are anymore
where is my daughter   where
has she gone

& when she says this
i swear for a moment i see yasmeen
flickering in the corner of the room
but i ignore her to instead turn
to my mother & snarl   *& where*
is my mom   i feel sometimes
like i got two ghost parents
before turning to slam the door
to my room

The Silence

i'm suspended from school for a week
my mother leaves for work in the morning
& i hear her come quietly home at dark
i have not spoken   or heard her speak
since i raised my voice that night

i spend hours imagining myself
as the other girl   yasmeen   not only the spirit-girl
who came to see me   but the one i built for years
myself   perfect in all the ways i am flawed
beautiful   bright & humming & full up
with laughter   beloved & blooming somewhere
kinder   where her language is her own
& unhunted   no one tells her to go back
where she came from   because she is home
& known & never disappears into the bathwater
isn't washed out by tears   & maybe i'm
all wrong not because i've come to the wrong
country   maybe any country on this side
of the membrane between worlds   isn't mine

& as if to confirm   my body starts its new & strange hum
as both my legs go abstract as static   my hips & stomach
& chest flicker in & out of color   my arms
i shift my weight & the plastic couch covering does not make
a single noise   remains silent as if completely
untouched   i check for a reflection in the dark surface
of the dormant television   & only the slightest outline

of a girl looks back   i call out   my voice hoarse
from disuse   *i'm ready now*   & wait for the jinn
to come fetch me   to shepherd me to the other side

i close my eyes & call again   heart beating in my throat
a moment passes   then another   & i open
to see my whole body restored   solid & human
& crackling the plastic on the couch

Alone

i thought haitham would call   & he hasn't
i imagine him   bright & laughing with his
real friends   & my loneliness grows teeth
i feel them chewing at my stomach

i miss my mother   i hear her moving
through the apartment   making only
the faintest sounds   thin stream of
running water   hushed sear of an egg
frying in butter   her soft step leaving
in the mornings   returning at dusk
murmuring to khaltu hala on the phone
& i ache   imagining haitham somewhere
in the apartment on the other end of the line

not a day passes without a plate
left on the counter when i emerge
from my room into the afternoon light
never a note or a knock   but always
without fail   a plate   & warm pita bread
in its basket   covered with a dishcloth
cut fruit in the refrigerator   curved slices
of pear   sometimes apple   today an orange
cold & thrilling & tart

i miss her voice   naming me   her small
& cool hands   her unlined girl-face
her rare & lilting laugh   i miss her younger
before i knew her   dancing in the photo

boundless & open & full of dreaming
dressed in color   jasmine blooms falling
from her neighborhood tree   to rest
beneath her feet   i mourn that girl & i miss
my mother   the only person i belong to
the one who chose me by choosing my name

Mama

i'm sorry i blamed you   i'm sorry
i yelled   i'm sorry you got this storm cloud
for a daughter instead of the flowers
you deserved   i'm sorry our life
is so small   i'm sorry   you didn't get
to be young   that you got me instead
i'm sorry you're alone   i'm sorry i'm
the only family you got to keep   i'm sorry
you lost your country & got one that doesn't
want us   i'm sorry you work all day & still
don't have anything for yourself   i'm sorry
on the days you wear the hat instead of
the scarf   & scared on the days you don't
i'm sorry you didn't get the daughter
you dreamt up   the girl named for
her sweetness & blooming   i'm sorry
you got me instead   & were left all alone
to raise me   i'm sorry my arabic
isn't better   i'm sorry for being so
american in here & not enough of one
out there   i'm sorry i blamed your scarf
when they called me a terrorist   i'm sorry
i blamed your loss for the ways my life
feels empty   i'm sorry for not making
you laugh enough   for never trying anymore
to make you smile   i'm sorry
you're lonely   i am too   i'm sorry
i'm not better company   i'm sorry
that i'm so gloomy   that i'm not

beautiful like you   i'm sorry for reminding you
of my father   for reminding you of what you lost
i'm sorry you made this life
for me   instead of the bright & bountiful one
you could have tried to make for only
yourself   i'm sorry i embarrass you
i'm sorry i don't have anything to show you
that it was all worth it   i'm sorry
i shouted at you   i'll say
when my mother gets home

Yasmeen

i've been in the bathtub so long i worry
something might take root
my fading fingers are graying & wrinkled
from the water   i chant my apology
to my mother out loud until i feel it
memorized   then hold my breath & slide
my body down the tub until my head
is underwater   & in the silence i decide
yasmeen is the daughter my mother
deserves   bright spot in her weary day
sprig of jasmine in her small life
something to be proud of   at last

i sit up in the tub & call her in every
way i can   first by name   shouting it
then chanting then with a plea   & still
she is not here   i remember the night
she appeared   the cassette & my closed
eyes   mama fatheya's warnings   *don't*
raise your voice or you will call them to
our side   & i sing   mouth open &
eyes shut   i gather all the lyrics i remember
& try to lure her again   نار يا حبيبي نار
اه يا حبيبي بحبك
& when i've exhausted all the words i know
to all the songs   i open my eyes
& still   she will not answer me

Haitham

my mother comes home & settles heavily
onto the couch   tired face in her hands

i sit next to her & begin   but it comes out
all wrong   out of order   *i'm sorry you got*

me as a daughter instead of the one   you deserve
i'm sorry i'm me   & not yasmeen   i'm sorry

& the telephone won't stop ringing   i falter
before i can finish   & before she says anything

she crosses to answer the call   *yes*
hi, khalti fatheya   what is it   what happened

a silence   then another   my mother
clamping her hand to her mouth

her eyes filling   still silent   *yes   we're coming*
we're coming now   & she fits the phone back

into its cradle   *get your jacket   what happened*
you have to get your jacket   where are we going

she will not answer & after she locks the door behind us
my mother cradles my face with her cold hands

we are going to the hospital   it's haitham

The Bus

the bus clatters down the crowded street   filled as always
to the brim with people   all of us in shades of brown
of sepia   & the smell packs tight around us   bodies
worked too hard & gone sour

i am standing with my silent mother   my distracted mother
swaying beside me & whispering a softest prayer under
her breath   her eyes distant & downcast   i miss her

& reach finally out to hold her hand   right then the bus
hits a bump in the pockmarked road   my mother's hand
pulls impossibly far away from mine   to grab the rail above
& i shove my fist deep into my pocket
shame hot against my throat

PART 2

OLD COUNTRY

Haitham

seems so small   crowded by machines
keeping him alive   i've never seen him
so still   so emptied of laughter   a rip
in his right cheek the length of a finger
sewn up in dark stitches   bandages winding
his forehead   tube inserted in the corner
of his cracked mouth

mama fatheya has not greeted us   has not
moved from her station at his bedside   leaning
heavily on her walking stick with one hand
prayer beads cabling through the other
while she recites a stream of indiscernible
language   i let my eyes blur & can
see it   pouring from her mouth like smoke
& absorbing into his body

behind me   his mother is sobbing to mine
my fault   i sent him to the bigala after dark
i should have kept him home   it isn't safe
not for any of us   he's only a little boy
& the story unfurls   a group of fully grown
men   circling him in the parking lot   taking
turns with their boots   with a bat   until
the shopkeeper   hearing the commotion
comes out with his shotgun   & scatters them
squats over haitham's broken body   groceries
smashed & scattered on the asphalt

& while he gathers up the boy   a brick
then another   goes crashing through the windows
of his store   & he tells haitham's stricken mother
*i don't understand   between blows   they were calling
him mohammed*

& i'm choking on the story   on the smells   on
the drone of prayers streaming from mama fatheya's
unmoving mouth   i can't bear to be in this building
full of dying   & push my way out of the room
my mother calling out behind me

Hala

the hospital is a maze   every room its own private
chamber of grief   i wander numbly through the stark halls
& as much as it hurts to see haitham like this   when he is
usually a clatter of movement   always a flurry of laughter
& talking & motioning with his hands   his face's hundred
cartoonish expressions   to see him motionless
the brokenness of his face
it hurts more to be away   the superstition
as always   arrives   to convince me he cannot die
as long as i'm in the room   & i turn back to find him

outside the door   my mother is sitting with khaltu hala
whose sobs have stilled   her eyes are haunted   staring into
some invisible point in space   the words pouring
from her mouth   *he's all i have*   *he's the only thing*
in this world that's mine   *it should have been me*   *i'd give*
anything for it to have been me instead   *i brought him here*
so we could have a different kind of life   *& even here i couldn't*
keep him safe   *so what was all of it for?*   *everything i lost*
it was all so i could give him a different life   *what if i lose*
him too?   & here her face crumples   her whole body
collapses into grief   my mother gathers her in her arms
& rocks her like a baby   & i wait for her to make
the empty   comforting promise   to say   *he'll be okay*
to say   *he'll wake up*   i want to hear it too
but she will not lie to her sobbing friend   instead she repeats
until it is almost a chant   *i know*   *i know*   *i know*

Touched

it's the last morning of my suspension & we are crowded
into the bus   my mother & i

pointed back toward the hospital

her face is far away   troubled   we have not eaten
since the night before   & i mean to leave her be

but i can't hold all this myself   *mama*   silence
mama   *what is it?*   *what will i do if he dies?*

the bus jolts to a stop   & a stranger   a man   is pushed
up against my mother   her face changes & she snarls

don't touch me   *don't you dare touch me*   & turns away
ignoring his flustered apology   she is silent a long time

then speaks without looking at me   her eyes in some
faraway place that hurts her   *there were officers*

they stopped us in our car & wanted   to touch me
there were so many of them   teeth shining in the dark

banging on the car windows with their guns   your father
he would not unlock the doors

& here her eyes empty entirely

when he tried to drive us away   they shot him
her eyes are large & tearless   hands clutching her coat

against her shrunken body   i cannot stand to hear the rest
of the story   my eyes are hot & my whole body is ringing

& i can't stand to be so near her open hurting   pushed into
her perfumed side by the crowd

so i shove my way through
the sour crush of bodies & off the bus

my mother's hoarse cry
my name   ripping through the air
sealed in by the closing doors

Running

my mother is screaming something i cannot hear
i hesitate & look to her through the window of
the moving bus   then turn & run down a block
crowded with pedestrians   ducking & turning
& crossing busy streets   i run until my lungs
are searing   my heart hammering & swollen
i look up & find myself in an unfamiliar part
of the city   & feel faint for want of water

just ahead   a cluster of tents & clamoring
& music   smells of charring meat   & clapping
& laughter & bells   for a moment i want
to go back to my mother   to apologize
to sit with her by haitham's bed & hold his hand

but my hunger heaves my tired body
toward the smell   into the festival
wetting my chapped mouth

Street Fair

i wander through the maze of color & smell
a parade running like a vein through the middle
& all around   i see booths draped in what looks
like every flag   i think for a second to look
for mine   & of course it is not there   mine
not a culture exciting enough for a booth   for a fair
only ever mentioned in a list of warnings on the news

at a stall draped in the same red white black green
as our flag   i ask for food   for water   the seller
names a price   i feel for my wallet & remember it
with a jolt   sitting untouched on the kitchen counter
& my armpits go damp with fear in the autumn chill

i turn away & am pulled   as if by water
into the current of dancers   musicians   horses
& the metallic trill of tambourines   throbbing of drums
& i cannot see anything but the bright rustle of skirts
of belled ankles   arms twisting up & heads
thrown back   the crowd pressing in closer
& pulling me along   my feet sometimes
not touching the ground

Houses

the parade releases me right as my lungs begin
to seize for air   i gasp & stumble into a quiet street
bent over & coughing   pulling the late autumn's
clean cold into my throat in ragged gulps   the minutes
pass & i heave myself upright   & take in the block ahead
gilded with bright foliage   scattering golden leaves
into the street   & onto the row of long staircases
leading up to each high house   each railing molded
in intricate patterns   grapevines   long-haired sirens
tiny metal flowers   the light in each window   warm
& thrumming with the satisfied lives inside

Trespassing

halfway down the block i hear the squeak
of an unlatched gate   swaying in the stirring
breeze   the leaves swirling upward in circles
from the pavement   the windows of the house
above   darkened & quiet

i have to keep moving   to outrun this day
this week   the sight of haitham's split mouth
taped to its tube   i push through the gate
& hear my heart pounding in my ears
muffling everything else   i pause   & my mother's
animal cry   *don't touch me   they shot him*
rips back into my thoughts   another step forward
& it disappears   the fleeting thought   *he's dead*
because of her   drowned by a warm wash of guilt
another step & it goes silent   i move unseeing this way
until i have turned from the side of the house
to its backyard   & see the enormous swimming pool
stretched across   its water warm & wafting steam
in little curls   into the air

The Water

before i can talk myself out of what is definitely
a stupid idea   i've undressed & lowered myself
into the water   searching for something like
the echoing peace of the bathtub at home   the pool
is colder than it looks & smells sharply of chlorine
i am not a good swimmer   but i can keep myself
generally afloat   & paddle a slow lap around the edge
then another   another   & finally   sucking in
a mouthful of air   i submerge my head
& force my eyes open against the sting

i blow a thick stream of bubbles into the blue quiet
& kick myself forward   barely moving before
i have to come up again for air   the world so loud
& violent in its color after the dark silence of the water
another intake of breath & i plunge again into
the quiet   propel myself forward with my clumsy
kicks   my graceless arms finding a strange music
in the water's weight   stretching forward then arcing
to my sides   every movement a victory
of my inelegant body   & the simple motion
soothes me   the guarantee that if i only kick
my legs   & pull with my arms   my body will
drive forward   every moment i raise my head
for air feels like an interruption   i swim this way
until my limbs feel emptied of their bones

Caught

so tired i feel   a little loosened
from my body   i crumple by the edge
of the pool & shiver   blotting myself
dry with the thick fleece   of my sweatshirt
i pile my clothes back on   my soaked hair
dripping a steady stream   down the nape
of my neck   the first actual fun i've managed
since fighting with haitham   though even
thinking his name   calls back the ache
& the tears grow hot in my chlorine-stung eyes
i stretch onto my back by the pool's edge   feeling
thoroughly sorry for myself   falling again into wishing
for another self   another life   until the distant
squeak of the gate opening   stills my whole
humming body into listening   waiting to be caught

an older man   hair graying around his ears
strides into the yard   a tiny limp dragging
his left foot a beat behind the other   & there is
no way he has not seen me   he stops just short
of the pool's edge   & bends at the waist
peering into the shimmering water   for anything
inside   i wince at his right foot   stepping
heavily on the ends   of my drenched hair
& look guiltily up into his face   his gray eyes
sliding unfocused across   then past

my splayed body   he shrugs   blows into
his thick hands for warmth   & makes his way
slowly back into the house   i sit up & glance
down at my body   & my body is not there

The Diner

i pull myself up from the tiled edge of the pool
& hurry out into the hushed street   i watch myself
flicker in & out   before finally going solid   i think
i have maybe just saved my own life   by being
unnoticeable   i want to figure out what
makes me disappear   what brings me back

i comb through my memories of disappearing
in the bathtub   at school   now at the edge
of a stranger's swimming pool   each time   i'd been feeling
that i didn't want to be myself   wishing for a different life
& the thought clicks loudly into place   i can disappear
by dwelling on the wish   that i was not here
that yasmeen had been born instead

by now my hunger is a sharp pang   heightened
by swimming & running   my eyes go in & out of focus
& when they blur over   i see new movement
figures disappearing when i blink & look again
strange birds   delicate & barely formed
twisting translucent through the air
solemn cats assembling silently up each staircase
covered in a layer of mist
another blink & they've cleared away   all except
the slightest outline of a girl   gliding halfway up
the block   away from me   yasmeen   she's come
back   i hurry along behind her   resisting
the urge to call out   in case she flickers away
& leaves me behind   she turns into another quiet street

& melts into the closed door of a small diner   i push
the door open & follow   & in the clatter of dishes
& talk   i know she's left me again   i have no money
& no plan & am governed now only by my hunger
so i tremble into a vinyl booth & ask the cheerful
lipsticked waitress for a cheeseburger   fries
a strawberry milkshake   mozzarella sticks   a slice
of apple pie   i down my first glass of water
in two gulps & ask for another   & when the food arrives
crowded onto my small table   i eat steadily without
coming up for air   until i am so full i feel a little sick

The Stranger

now that i've eaten & can think clearly i understand
how much trouble i am about to get into   i maybe
could have wheedled   a free plate of fries   some water
from the kind waitress   with my sad story
& empty pockets   but how to ask for an entire feast
after i've already eaten it

to buy myself some time i ask for the menu again
pretend to study it while she clears my round
of greasy plates
my heart is knocking loudly around my body & any
minute now i am going to cry   i close my eyes
& before i can open them   a man's voice
so close he must be at my table   asks me if i am all right

my eyes spring open & he is sitting across from me
his eyes are large & pouched   sad but not unkind
their sharp blue not unlike pool water   stark in their
dim & bloodshot whites   he's the age i imagine
my father to be   though his gray-brown mustache
is wispy   & his beard missing in patches   like
the new growths of the boys at my school   but his
suit looks expensive   his fingernails short & clean
& polished   & when the waitress approaches
he hands her two bills from a roll he produces   & bares
his gray teeth in a smile that does not quite reach his eyes
that will be all for my niece & just a coffee for me   cream

& three sugars   *thanks*   she leaves
& he turns the gray smile to me   asks again
if i'm okay   & do i need help getting home

i close my eyes again   mama's voice   my whole life
never go anywhere alone with a man   *not even*
the next room   *not even*   *an uncle or cousin*   *not even*
& in a prickle of tears i realize why   & swat her voice
from my head before the first drop falls   i am so tired
i just want to go home   i just want
i am so full of wanting   so much of it for what i cannot
change   again haitham's broken face
again my mother's shriek   *they shot him*   i am so tired
of everything happening to me at once   he seems
nice enough   & i want so badly
to go home   i open my eyes & nod

The Stranger

i fumble with my seat belt while the engine wheezes
awake   i've given him my address   i'm so tired
& just want to go home   his car is too hot
& smells like old meat   something sweetly rotting
i peel off my thick sweatshirt & fold it into my lap

he has not spoken & my skin prickles with his looking

at a red light he turns to me   his teeth glinting wetly
in a smile   & murmurs   so quietly i can barely hear him
you have a beautiful neck   & turns back to face
ahead when the light changes   i feel
knotted & embarrassed by the compliment
& put my sweatshirt back on

the neighborhoods crawl past the windows of the car
not one of them mine   or anything i recognize
after another turn the highway stretches endless before us
the sun setting in a riot of color & fire

i do not want to make him upset   but i know now
that this is not the way home   i wet my chapped lips
& squeak out a pitiful   *excuse me*   & he does not turn
i clear my throat & try it louder   when he faces me
i speak very slowly   to keep the tremble in my voice
at bay   *excuse me, hi, if you'd like i can try & give you
directions? i don't think this is, i mean, i'm not
sure but i don't think this is the right way?*   & he smiles
kindly & says gently   *oh, of course, no, i know,
it's just that you live a few towns over*   & before i can finish
exhaling in relief   he continues   *so i thought we'd check into
a hotel   & do the rest of the trip in the morning*
& i feel like i've swallowed my own sinking heart

The Driveway

he steers the car into the circular driveway of a hotel
hands his keys to a young man dressed in dark blue velvet
& motions me in through the revolving door   tells me
to hang back while he handles the room
& when he's gone i look frantically around for help
but everywhere i look i see men & more men & i cannot
risk one worse than the one that brought me

i feel a hand on my arm   my body already on high alert
as i turn   ready to use my teeth   my nails   the hand
is not quite solid   not quite warm   humming
beneath the surface with something i can't name
& before i can speak she begins
& the voice in her mouth is like mine   the hand
on my arm exactly like mine   *you have to go   now*
get on that bus   & all my questions root me
to the spot   her eyes are large & urgent
are my eyes   yasmeen   more solid than i've ever
seen her   motions again   frantically   & when i still
do not move   she turns   hurries down
the driveway   & climbs into a small bus marked
AIRPORT SHUTTLE   & in an instant i am unfrozen
adrenaline coursing through my shaking limbs   as i move
to follow her   i slip quietly
back out through the revolving door   hurry toward the bus
the driver   smoking a cigarette on one side   does not
see me climb in through the open door on the other
& inside yasmeen has disappeared once more

i crawl into the very last row & cower   as the shuttle
fills in sparsely with passengers   though no one
sits in the back or sees me crouched in the dark
my face pressed into the smell of leather   blood roaring
in my ears   she's real   & she saved me   & i need her
to come back   the driver finishes his cigarette
& climbs cheerfully on board
& the shuttle glides off into the night

The Airport

at the airport the crowd swirls busily around me
i barely avoid being flattened by a luggage cart
& an irritated woman asks me to *please move*   her
please pronounced like a threat   i scurry into
an empty corner to think   & hear a familiar note
of arabic in the air   then another   i look up
& the counter in front of me is crowded with
my people   carts piled high with taped-up
suitcases   & overflowing shopping bags   mothers
draped in bright fabrics clamping rowdy children
to their sides   a small boy is wailing   angry tears
spouting down his face   while his father tries
to soothe him   *you'll love it back home   wait*
until you meet your cousins   your grandparents
& see the river   & eat the sweetest guava
you'll ever taste   i'll teach you how to climb trees
how to swim   you'll see   you are going to be
so happy   & with a pang i miss my mother

Broken Arabic

i spot a stooped woman   mama fatheya's age
seated to the side in a wheelchair   while her family
checks their bags   i approach   not realizing
i'm speaking in english   until she shakes her head
& repeats in her gravelly voice   *only arabic*

in my clumsy arabic i try to explain   that i need
help getting home   that i'm all alone & afraid
& don't know who can help me   i stumble
through the sentences   pausing to remember
each word   & finally the only sentence i can assemble
is *i want to go home   i want to go home*

where is your mother?   she asks   concerned
& through my tears i blubber wetly   *at home*
are you here all alone?   & i nod   *& you don't*
have any way of getting home?   & i shake my head
& in the mess i've made with my broken arabic
she calls to her daughter   *this poor child*
wants to go home   we have to help her   & i don't
realize that i've mixed up the words   & the word
for *home* i'd been using this whole time   was *homeland*

No Daughter

the younger woman   puts one hand   on my shoulder
nails stained red-brown with henna
smooths my hair with her other palm
& asks   *do you speak arabic?*
still flustered by the spreading chaos i've made
with my half language   i shake my head no
she clicks her tongue in disapproval   & turns to speak
to the older woman   *look at her hair   the dirty clothes*
i don't think this girl belongs to anyone   no daughter of mine
no girl i named   would ever be allowed out looking
like this   she must not have a family   at least not one
that she matters to   & i feel shame like bile rising sour
in my throat   she looks over to me & smiles
while continuing   through gritted teeth   to her mother
stupid child doesn't even speak arabic   & all my rage
all my frustration   my exhaustion   my fear   fill me
to bursting   my arabic finds me & i hiss
up into her widening eyes   *i have a mother*
i belong to someone   i belong   before i turn
on my heel & storm away   & see yasmeen
again   flickering in & out of the crowd
headed for the elevator

The Elevator

i ram a button to summon the service elevator
out of places to go so i'm following yasmeen
& i want to track her down
to ask her to help me again   the metal doors
slide open   & shut once i'm inside
& she is not there

& in the silver quiet i feel the exhaustion soak
my body   & i feel homesick for the confines
of the apartment   safe from this enormous world
& its horrors   i want to go home   i want
to find my way home   the elevator has not moved
i want to go home   i push the button to open the doors
deciding instead to find the stairs   the doors part
in a surge of warm air   outside the airport is gone

& in its place is the photograph of my parents
life-sized   & real with smells & dry expansive heat
everything still frozen in its place   my mother
laughing & dancing & in love   my father   his hand
mere moments from her waist   so close i can see
the sweat beading his brow   the mosquito
a second from his neck   my father's dark hair
lush & dense & coiled   flimsy cotton of his shirt soaked
in sweat   little gap in his front teeth   & the look
in his eyes   dazed by his good luck

yasmeen steps into the frame   & she looks fully
human   solid & actually walking   instead
of her usual supernatural glide   from this close
we're not so different   she looks like me dressed
in costume   with better grooming & better posture   but still
me   extends her hand & says   *are you coming?*
& when i take it her hand is solid & warm   a real
pulse   full of real blood

The Photograph

we step into the party at the exact moment
my father's hand meets my mother's waist
& pulls her closer to him   her laugh rings out
& soaks into the music   the night black
as velvet but for the glow of fairy lights strung
across the trees   the air smells green & floral
& in the distance   the faintest smell of smoke

after a few songs i tear my eyes reluctantly
from my parents to take in the other guests
at a table playing cards i spot khaltu amal   unbleached
& smiling   her hair fastened in two skinny braids

& leaned up against a jasmine tree   mostly hidden
by its branches   is haitham's mother   khaltu hala
twisting a pearl ring around her index finger &
joking slyly with a man whose face is exactly
haitham's   & just beyond them on a makeshift
rickety stage   the band pours its song into the night
the drummer   my arabic teacher   lanky
& with a full afro of hair restored   tie loosened
around his neck   on the keyboard is abbas
who drives the bus   & leaned up against
the microphone   crooning into it like a lover
barely recognizable in his joy   is the man who runs
the bigala   though here his face is unlined
& without its signature scowl   they all look
so happy   so young & full of what is possible

how could they ever have left   why couldn't i
have been born into this version of us   have
grown up being sung to   swung from arm
to loving arm by both my parents   by their friends
everyone still alive   shining in the heat   back home

Home

at first i think i must be dreaming   or making it
all up   but i walk across the garden & feel the grass
crunching beneath my feet   i put my hands
against a date palm   & its trunk is warm & rough
to my touch   & in front of me is a jasmine tree
its flowers blooming & perfume heady & sweet
& when i reach for one it comes away easily into my hand

i could spend hours just watching my parents dance
watching the muscles animating my father's living face
but i feel tugged toward the exit by my other longing
i slip through the clanging metal gate   my lost country
just outside

Home

on the quiet street outside i mark the site
of the party by its muffled sounds   then turn
a corner & find myself walking along the river
rippling in the darkness   the aching notes
of the call to prayer   echoing out
from a minaret nearby   & before i can finish
catching my breath   i feel a hand on my back
a waft of scent   what might be sesame & a flower
whose name i never learned   & i look up to see
yasmeen beside me   my own awe reflected
in her widened eyes   the eyes exactly mine   my gratitude
makes me awkward & i do not look at her as i murmur
thank you for helping me   & the hand is on my arm again
solid this time as she replies   *of course*

& i don't know what else to say so we are silent for a while
before she speaks again   *have you heard that saying*
"there but for the grace of god go i"   & i shake my head
it's basically, like, that could have been me, you know?
& that's what i would have wanted someone to do for me so—
& as she says this i can't believe i haven't already asked
so i interrupt   *wait, so, are you me?*   & i know
it sounds stupid as i say it   & i already feel
the warm spread of shame   but she doesn't laugh
& she doesn't say no   instead she bites her lip in thought
well, i'm yasmeen she begins

which, by the way, hi   here a small smile   *so, we're parallel*
versions of each other   *like, you're me if something different*

were to happen somewhere in the story   & it's like i've always
imagined   i know the answer before i even ask
but still i ask   *in your version, is baba alive?*   she nods
& mama fatheya's voice comes back to me   clear
as a recording   *one child for each world*
& i am tripping over myself with questions

enough that i don't register the hollowness of her answers
*is he amazing?   yes   is mama happy?   all the time
do you have a lot of friends?*   her face makes an expression
i can't name & for a moment she looks nothing like me   *sure
what are their names? what are they like?   just some girls
from arabic class. they're nice   & haitham?*   & instead
of answering she turns the line of questioning on me
do you also collect cassettes?   & i can't contain my excitement
oh my god, yes, you too?   & she laughs in recognition
yes! what's your favorite? i love the sayed khalifa one
& immediately we are singing the line in unison
يا عقد اللولي   لولي
يا بنت يا حلوة يا لولي

& for a moment all my questions are forgotten
my racing head quieted by this moment of kinship
i sit awhile in the feeling as yasmeen peers
into the river   lost in some thought of her own until i ask
have you been here before?   & she shakes her head
only in dreams & old pictures   & she says it exactly like
i would have   & even though she already knows
i turn to face her   reach to shake her hand   then decide
it would be weird so i pull my hand back & wave

you probably know this already but it feels weird not to say
hi, i'm nima   she smiles   & i watch my face in hers
my smile stretching into hers   but the eyebrows
are less unruly & the hair is plaited neatly into a thick
untousled braid   & i can't help but ask   *how do you get*
your hair to do that? to stay put?   & she smiles again
sesame oil & edge control   as i will myself to remember
all of it   this not-dream   this country   this other girl
together we stand at the riverbank   & watch the moon
float over the water   illuminating the city in ghostly colors

Haitham

we walk back into the thrum of the party
& i don't know who i want to follow first
my parents still dancing & whispering
to one another   bright center in the knot
of dancers   but my attention is caught
once again by the man leaned up against
the tree with khaltu hala   haitham's
disappeared father   living & gesturing wildly
with his hands as he talks in the exact manner
of haitham   his wiry frame & big teeth

walking next to me as we approach them
yasmeen whispers   *it's amazing how he looks*
exactly like haitham   & i don't think
to ask how she knows haitham's face
haitham's name   if he's there in her version
of the story   too shocked myself
by the resemblance   the face i know
better than my own   fastened onto
this one i've never seen   haitham's father
absent from any photograph   haitham's father
whose name he never says   khaltu hala never says
mama fatheya never says   & here he is
smelling of cinnamon & sweat   running
his thumb across the ring on hala's finger
until a voice calls out   *ashraf! how are*
you, man?   & he pulls his hand away

as if bitten   steps a respectful distance
from khaltu hala   & turns to greet his friend
while hala slinks off into the dancing crowd
shame twisting itself in her face

Ashraf

torn between following khaltu hala
back to my parents   & haitham's
mystery father   the story written
in their secrecy   i give in to my curiosity
& inch closer to hear him chatting
with his friend   *work's fine,*
you know, same old, never thought
i'd end up working for the government
but, you know   & his friend cuts in
we understand you have mouths
to feed   how are the kids? your wife?

& i work to unscramble these facts
in my knotted brain   kids   a wife
who it is clear now was not hala
& haitham never mentioned having siblings
never mentions his father at all
despite the life he spends wearing that man's
exact haunted face

Visitors

i walk   dazed   back into the knot of dancers
& just as i reach out to touch my mother's arm
yasmeen grabs my wrist   *stop   she can't*
see you   we're only visitors, you understand?
we're not part of this part of time   you'll only
scare her   & i pull my hand back to my side

then why are we here? does this mean we can't stay?
& in her face i watch my features soften   almost
as if with pity   *i think we're just supposed*
to watch   to learn something   maybe fill in
some of the gaps we both have   answer some
of the questions, you know?   & something in my gut
is telling me there's more   but i nod   watching
khaltu hala approach my mother   her jaw hardened
to keep the tears in   yasmeen moves closer
to listen   & i will too   but first i steal an open
hungry stare into my father's living face   before yasmeen
tugs on my hand & motions for us to follow
as my mother & khaltu hala
walk to a quiet corner of the party

aisha, i'm pregnant   hala whispers
as understanding arranges itself first onto
my mother's face   then panic   *oh, hala   oh no*

after finally submitting to an embrace   hala turns
to go home   refusing my mother's offer for company
i'm tired   i'll call you in the morning
& leaves my mother to sit alone with the news
worry creasing her face
hands absently finding her stomach
i haven't told anyone yet, but so am i

Haitham

never talks about his father   even when we were little
the contract was wordless & understood   the contract
i broke & i am afraid i've broken everything along with it

i wonder how much he knows about this man whose face
he wears   i wonder if he knows how alike their features are

their laugh   their electric darting movements   i wonder

if he ever feels unwanted   if it hurts him to hear me
rhapsodize about my immortalized father   while never asking
about his dreams of his   i wonder if he thinks about him

what he thinks about him   i wonder if he's still alive
haitham's father   where he lives
i will not let myself wonder

if haitham is still alive   if i'll ever see him again

The Lesson

khaltu amal   who i guess is not my khaltu yet   just amal
a bride-to-be   stands facing my mother   not yet

my mother   just aisha   in the newly gathered circle
of women   some accompanied by drums

some clapping their two hands   aisha dances & amal
tries to mirror her movements   but cannot catch

the drumbeat   my mother stops   & works to rearrange
amal's posture   just as she does with mine

back arched   arms pulled back at the shoulder
like resting wings   chin tilted skyward

try it again   from the waist this time, not the legs   slowly
good!   now faster   & as the dance arranges itself

into amal's formerly graceless body   i see her face light up
in a smile   not the strained grimace i've seen her wearing

all my life   this one reaches her eyes & glows
& together she & aisha fall into step   the others rising

from their chairs to join them   one of them calls
to my mother   *aisha   graceful one   they should have*

named you نِعْمَة   *nima   grace*   & my mother laughs
it's too late to change mine   but maybe i'll save it for my daughter

The Lovers

the band plays its final soaring note   & the party
releases its clamor of guests   they pile into cars & onto
motorcycles   & i try to memorize each face before
it absorbs back into history

my parents   hand in hand   set off on foot
& walk the wide road along the river
their chatter soft in the cooling air   yasmeen & i
hurrying behind them   trying to get close enough
to hear   my mother's voice floats toward us
i think it's a girl   *a daughter*   her small hands
unchanged by the years   touching her stomach in awe

& though his face creases a little   in an expression
i do not know   i quickly forget
because for the first time   i am hearing
my father's voice   deep & throaty
a pleasant growl   wrapping itself around
my mother's name in wonder   in disbelief
& with a whoop of excitement
he picks his beloved up by the waist   their child
piecing together inside   he spins her around
until they are both dizzy & helpless with laughter

Yasmeen

my parents just ahead of us   walking hand
in hand & content   the hot air
like a woolen blanket   thick & comforting
even with the sweat glossing my brow
prickling in my armpits   i turn to yasmeen
i have so many questions for you
i don't even know where to start
& she smiles   *me too. can i go first?*
i nod & spend the rest of the walk answering her
about school & arabic class & my mother & haitham
& mama fatheya & khaltu hala   about all
the contours of my small life   the photographs
& old songs i collect   i tell her about my loneliness
my mother's loneliness   & i even
with a little pang of embarrassment   tell her
about the music videos   about dancing
& the way it makes me feel to forget my body
to imagine it freer & full of grace
& she listens   rapt   nodding & exclaiming
& asking more questions   & it feels so good
to feel so interesting   to be attended to
in her unblinking way   & now my father is reaching
for the gate & i haven't gotten to ask yasmeen
a single question of my own

The House

we arrive outside a whitewashed house
where my father unlocks the gate

inside   a tiled courtyard scattered
with potted flowers   gnarled cacti

walls carpeted in bougainvillea
a jasmine tree   thickly perfuming the air

my grandmother   her face rounded
like my mother's   hair still dark & streaked

with gray   parted in two heavy braids
coiled around her ears   waters the flowers

in her nightgown   raises an eyebrow as the gate
swings open to let my parents inside

though her voice is full of mirth when she calls
home so early?   & her daughter

& new son smile back   she sets down her watering can
& labors to her feet   bemoans her creaking knees

seated at the kitchen table   over plates
of spiced beans   sheep's cheese & charred

puffs of bread   my mother shyly reveals
her news   her mother's ululating wakes the cats

& they slink   unimpressed   into the yard

Morning

my parents set off for bed & i fall into
a dreamless sleep   right there
at the kitchen table   arms folded to pillow
my racing head   & wake to sunlight
like i've never seen   so bright   so saturated
it is almost a pigment   almost the color
of marigolds   & before i can convince myself
i've dreamt the whole thing   yasmeen's voice
calls out behind me   *you know you snore,*
right?   i turn to see her   crisp & uncrumpled
& polished   & as i open my mouth to ask
if she'd even slept   a movement outside the window
catches my eye   my grandmother   awake
& feeding the birds   & in this perfect morning light
i see so much of my face in hers   i almost think to love it

The Photographs

i wander out of the kitchen to explore the rest
of the quiet house   its cool stone floors

its every wall hung heavy with pictures   creased
with age & soft in gray tones   men in neat suits

& cylindrical hats   each one jaunty with its tassel
men in crisp white tunics   a turban winding each head

& most of all   photographs crowded with women
covered & uncovered   some in sundresses

flared around the ankle   enormous sunglasses
beehives & bouffants & big curls & coiffed waves

some swathed from neck to ankle in tobes   their colors
lost to time & the gray scale of the camera

all of them my people   all of them unknown
i peer into each face & feel   for the first time

that i belong to other people   my face just a collage
of all their faces   & beyond the gray of the photos

i swear i see my exact shade of brown   my exact
eyes   each exact coil of my hair   inherited

from the bodies in these photographs   & now
my body   mine   my turn with these features

i turn to find yasmeen beside me   gazing into these same
photographs   hunger in her upturned face

Yasmeen

moved by the ache in yasmeen's eyes   & knowing
she must see it echoed in mine   i put my hand on her arm
i don't know how else to explain this connection i feel to
the girl with my face   who longs for what i long for
whose smile is my smile   & i am brimming with questions
where do you live?   where did you grow up?
do you know how you got your name?   she skips over
the first two & gets right to the name   *it's honestly so dumb*
mama just likes the flower   that's it   i always wished
i'd gotten your name instead   one that actually
means something   & through her eyes my name takes on
a new polish   like i am finally
holding it up to the light

Room

a song wafts down the stairs & yasmeen & i
pull ourselves from the moment to follow it

in a small room painted pool-water blue   my parents
still in their party clothes   are sprawled across
their unmade bed

staring up at the lazy turns of the ceiling fan   their fingers
interlaced   laughter & chatter interrupted
only to change the song

to remark   *i love this one*   & sing along to a few words
the room is cluttered   records stacked on every surface

books balanced between them   some tented open
to mark a page

my mother sits up   cross-legged
on the patterned bedspread

do you think it's too early to call hala?   i'm worried about her
& just then   as if summoned   the telephone
on the bedside table

starts to ring   my father answers   listening intently
answering only in short syllables   *yes   where?   okay*

puts the receiver back into its cradle as he stands   shoving
his feet into shoes   buttoning his shirt   he tosses

a simple gray scarf to my mother & says   his voice strained
let's go   it's hala   they caught her with ashraf last night

alone in his car

they've been detained   the charge is adultery

Hala

we idle in the car outside a large white house
with blue shutters   until another car arrives

screeching to a halt   & a younger mama fatheya   draped
in a brightly patterned tobe   steps out

partway through what must have been a much longer speech
our whole family's reputation   your father will be

the laughingstock of the university   & how am i ever supposed
to show my face again   i can't believe you'd be so stupid

what would you have done   if i hadn't happened to have american
dollars for the bribe   maybe it would have served you right if i'd

just left you to rot in that cell with that shameful boy
to serve out your sentence   i should be hearing

some thanks   some gratitude   some kind of apology
khaltu hala sits unmoving on the passenger side

her hair   which last night was long & lush   thick with kink
& curl   now shorn close against her skull

a bruise blooming over her left eye   i feel already
full of seeing   already the full weight of everything

i was never told   everything that was kept from me
i turn to yasmeen & see   my own shock mirrored in her face

Hala

inside the house is large & airy   cool stone floors
gauzy curtains softening the blazing sun outside

mama fatheya retreats to her room   her anger searing
& silent except for the eloquent slam of her bedroom door

in her own room khaltu hala sits bolt upright   her eyes
bloodshot & tearless   beneath the uneven shear of her hair

my mother sits beside her   stricken   & in the twitch
of her hand i see her deciding whether or not she can touch

her friend   what comfort she can muster in the face
of this great rupture   moments pass & finally

aisha exhales   reaches her hand & rests it gently
on hala's shoulder   & the stillness is broken

& hala crumples   with an unearthly howl
into my mother's lap   & in an echo of the scene

i last remember them in   my mother gathers her
into her arms & rocks her in that familiar chant

i know   *i know*   *i know*

my father hovers in the doorway   his posture unsure
& when hala starts to cry he averts his eyes

& does her the kindness of slipping wordlessly
from the room   my mother catches his eye

in his retreat   mouths *thank you*

Baba

we leave my mother to comfort khaltu hala
while yasmeen & i follow my father through his day

i can't help but ache   watching his face   moving & full
of muscle   replacing the frozen one i've memorized

from the photos   we follow him   & i learn the long gait
of his walk   his tall & wiry frame   his scent

of apples & smoke   he stops at a small cafe   packed
with men drinking tea & shouting & playing backgammon

at a table crowded with his friends he is greeted
with a cheer   *ahmed!*   & i feel tears in my throat

at the sound of his name   almost lost to time
my mother never says it   hardly ever

speaks of him & when she does   refers to him
only as   *your father*   my father   ahmed

sprawls into a chair & lights the cigarette he pulls
from behind his ear   his eyes thick-lashed & alert

as he listens to story after story   though he keeps
mostly quiet   he keeps hala's secret   keeps the news

of the baby   of me   a secret   & though he laughs
at every joke   & though i am barely acquainted

with his face   its movements & its moods   i think i see
a tightness in the smile   but i don't know what to name it

Baba

as the table starts to empty   my father rearranges
his long limbs & orders a glass of tea   it arrives

with a thick snowfall of sugar at the bottom of the cup
he stirs   looks into its amber depth & sighs

his eyebrows   thick & unruly as mine
knit together while he wrestles with some thought

that troubles him   his forehead furrowing   tea cooling
& undrunk   a man i recognize from the party joins him

apologizes for being late   motions to the waiter
for another glass of tea   & settles comfortably

into one-sided chatter with my father
the price of oil   the price of bread   his wife

aching for a child   that will not come   some friends
thinking of leaving for england   others for egypt

saudi arabia   canada   he claps my father jovially
on the shoulder   *why don't you & the wife come with us?*

soon there won't be any work left here
for anyone   & i hear you get used to the cold

my father tries & fails to force a smile   his face breaks
& i listen   holding my breath   ready for the pieces

to finally fit into place   the story of why we left our country
our home   & even america takes on a new luster

at the thought that baba chose it for us
that we were all meant to go together

to call a new country our home

The Coward

instead i watch my father tell his friend
that he is going to leave my mother

& he is going to leave me   though i can barely
hear him over the throb of my own sinking heart

the roar of blood in my ears   *i'm not ready*
i'm not   i love her   i do   i just always thought

i'd get to be young a little longer   maybe see the world
i've never even left this city   this country   & now we're having

this child   & i don't think i want that   i guess i never
thought my life would get   so small   so soon   a child?

with what money? what house?   she wants all three
of us crowded into that room? all three of us sleeping

in her childhood bed? in her childhood home?
& doesn't care how that makes me look   how it makes me feel

all of it   it's embarrassing   i hoped we were going to get out
of this country   people have started to go missing   & now

the soldiers everywhere   the raids   we could have tried
to leave & live a different kind of life   & now we're stuck

his friend studies him   blows on his tea & takes a sip
so you come with us   do you already have a passport?

140

Mama

as my father plans the details of his escape   i drink in
one last look at his weak face   to replace the picture

in my mind   in the photographs   & my heart
hurts again & again for my mother   twirled in the street

by the coward she loves   off imagining names
for the daughter she was always going to raise alone

& i feel stupid   ashamed of the life i spent pining
for this stranger   this man i never knew   who never

wanted to know me   this ghost i've measured my mother
against   & now i know him   & i know he was never mine

to miss   even if he'd lived   mama was always
going to be alone

i mourn her as i've come to know her   always tired

unpinning her scarf after a long day at work   to sleep alone
& wake up alone & do all of it over again

i turn to yasmeen   *is this why i was sent here?*
to find out he never wanted me?   to find out he was never

going to be there   even if he'd lived?   & again
a pang for my mother   who i've spent my whole life

thinking of as half of an incomplete whole   as my other
parent instead of my only   yasmeen still has not spoken

so i continue   *i think i'm supposed to see this*
to know that mama was always going to be all i had

to know that mama was always enough   i feel the depth
& shape of my love for my mother   in a wash of tears

& i need to see her again   even this version
who is not yet mine

The Game

together yasmeen & i return to the house to find aisha
in the small living room   carefully peeling a grapefruit

its bright smell filling the air   she is draped across
a woven bed arranged with others around the room

a few mismatched chairs pulled in from other rooms
of the house for her gathering of friends

lazy hum of the ceiling fan above   flies orbiting
like little moons   the room smells sweetly of incense

& behind it the sharper scent of new paint   a bowl of dates
is passed around   each one wrinkled & leathery

in its caramel sweetness   i take in the carved wooden
shutters   ghostly light almost bursting behind them

my grandmother bustles about the younger women
soft flesh of her full upper arms   hair oiled & brushed

to a shining ripple   a fat braid coiled around each ear
henna black on her fingers & toes

henna a crimson highlight in her hair   reddest
at the neat parting   & two long scars burned ceremonially

down each of her cheeks   an adornment from
a forgotten time

as we approach i hear my mother musing to khaltu hala
i love the idea of naming her nima   but ahmed loves

the name yasmeen & you know   it's my favorite flower
it'll remind me of mama's garden   mama likes it too

says a daughter is an apple in her father's eye
& a flower in her mother's hair   she laughs

& shakes her head   & i go warm at the thought
of my name as mama's first choice

yasmeen is my father's daughter   the father
i never needed

khaltu amal   though not the one being spoken to
pipes up   *yasmeen is the prettier name, aisha, no question*

& khaltu hala rolls her eyes   her dislike for amal flavoring
the air around them   & if only to be contrary

she shoots back   *there's a guava tree in the garden too*
& i don't hear you trying to name the baby jawaafa

or after the doum tree or the lemon tree   i think nima
has more character   she stares at amal

as she pronounces this last word
someone produces a deck of cards   *why don't we make*

a game of it?   & with a smirk amal takes the cards
& starts to shuffle   *if i win a round, that's one point for yasmeen*

you win a round & it's a point for nima   my mother is quiet
at first   wary   then her face clears & she claps her hands

it'll be fun! best three out of five? but just for fun, okay?
i turn to catch yasmeen's eye but her face is stricken

i reach to touch her shoulder & she shrugs my hand away
& i am stung by her small rejection   as the game begins

they're playing concan   with speed & concentration
i've never seen   not the clumsy & laughing way haitham & i

play it with mama fatheya   who cheats shamelessly
gets up in the middle of the game to make tea

& loses half her cards in the couch cushions
amal's jaw is set   hala's brow is furrowed

they play entirely in silence   & with a grin amal sets down
a winning hand   & hala makes a frustrated noise

from the back of her throat as amal caws
one point for yasmeen!   & i feel that old hum in my body

yasmeen gasps & i follow her pointing hand
down to my feet   except my feet are not there

& fear slices through me   but before i can do anything
hala is shuffling the cards again

& the hum leaves my body   my feet flicker back into place
as they begin the next round   which hala wins

in just a few brutal moves   slaps down her cards
& calls out   *nima!*   & yasmeen's arm is instantly gone

dread settles onto her face until the cards are shuffled again
& her arm blurs back into sight

the next round is longer   tense   & finally
with a grunt   hala wins again   yasmeen's body

dissolving from the waist down   fearful tears pooling
in her eyes   & remaining there   even as the cards

are once again shuffled & her legs are restored
when amal wins the fourth round & i feel the ominous hum

in my body again   i cast about in panic for a way
to stop the game   i reach for the cards   but have

no hands to grab them with   & in a final surge
of desperation   i aim my foot at the tea set

arranged beside the group   mint leaves steeping
in a beautiful ornate ceramic pot   & kick the entire tray over

onto the cards   boiling tea splashing into khaltu amal's lap
her howl of pain   the game forgotten

as the women scramble to their feet

what have you done?   yasmeen hisses   jogging
to catch up as i stride toward the gate

i feel unsettled & afraid   something nagging at me
that i can't name   & i need somewhere quiet to think

Quiet

yasmeen pulls me by the hand before the sob escapes
my throat   & leads me outside into the blazing day
& for a moment the noise washes over me
muffling the feeling

cars clatter by in a honking of horns & cough of exhaust
sharing the street with bleating animals   pedestrians
crossing without looking to either side   escaping narrowly

with their lives   children crowd the car windows   hawking
bags of peanuts   sweet ropes of creamy white jasmine
& an old man whizzes past on a bicycle
barely missing yasmeen

who once again tugs at my hand   *if we don't move out*
of the way we're going to get flattened
& it's true that everything feels too loud   too bright
i just need a quiet place to think

i call to yasmeen over the commotion   *i need a quiet place*
to think   & yasmeen walks us in the direction of the river
to the skeleton of an unfinished building
a monster of gray concrete

its windows without glass   like sockets missing their eyes
on a raised bit of land flush against the river   its brilliant
blue   *wait*   i hesitate   *i didn't mean, like,*
abandoned-building quiet

don't be stupid   she replies   & she's pulling me along again
into the building   up one crumbling set of stairs   *yasmeen,*
where are we going? i should probably tell you now that i don't

love heights   as we climb another set of stairs   *hold on,*
would you stop for a second? shouldn't we talk about what
just happened?   without turning she calls back

here's this whole country we never got to see   don't you want to
see everything?   i feel the sweat prickling in my armpits
i can already see everything through this window
why don't we just stop here?

& she shakes her head   *the roof   i want to see everything*

A Country

i stumble   coughing   behind her onto the roof   & before
i can slow my breath i feel it catch again in my throat
as i look out & see it   the whole city   the desert just beyond it
our whole country panoramic before us   all the noise
softened by distance

i can just make out the sounds coming from a nearby minaret
a full-throated call to prayer   below us the world is rendered
in every variation of brown   sudden shocks of other
colors   bougainvillea planted everywhere   glossy green
of palm leaves   & as the sun begins to set the colors seem
almost painted   almost liquid   true pink   true orange
gold   its magentas & oranges like fruit
i long to touch it to my lips

yasmeen & i are silent   surrounded by what could
have been ours   the street below wafting its perfumes
of car exhaust   of corn & peanuts roasting
that ever-shifting smell of smoke
& for a moment i can forget my fear   the memory
of my vanishing body   how easily my name
could have been taken

instead i take in the colors   the smells   blue & gold
& unnamed sepia tones around us   streets bustling
with my people   with my family   yasmeen beside me
squeezing my hand

Yasmeen

as the panic from the game leaves my body
i remember   with a jolt   why we'd gone back to the house

yasmeen, we have to tell mama that baba is leaving her
you don't understand what it's like   her whole life

is like a shrine to him   she has to know what he
was really like   i turn to her   *wait, but in your life*

they're together, right? what's he like? what changed?
her face takes on a hunted look & she will not meet my eyes

i feel desperate   *why aren't you answering me? yes or no?*
are they together?   we need a plan

maybe i could write her a letter

or whisper to her in her sleep   or   & yasmeen shakes
her head   *we're not really here, remember?   i already*

told you, they can't see us   they can't hear us either
& i do remember   yasmeen telling me at the party

we're only visitors, you understand? we're not part
of this part of time   & i want to know why she knows

all this & i don't   *yasmeen, what are you not telling me?*
how do you know all this?   & how come i don't?

& the hunted look returns to her face   i've caught her
in some kind of lie   & i feel betrayed by everyone

my father making plans to make a life without me   & now

this girl i've grown secretly to think of as my sister   this girl
who brought me here   i remember her   leading me
through that day   that already feels so far away

to the diner   to the airport   into the scene
of the photograph   into this world

yasmeen, what are we doing here?

Half Possible

yasmeen sets her mouth in a hard line   & just as i think
she isn't going to tell me   she begins   *there is only meant*

to be one of us   & something tightens in my stomach
what do you mean?   she takes a step closer

you just saw it for yourself   *there is no stupid parallel universe*
our mother has one daughter & that daughter has one name

my stomach begins to twist itself into a knot   as i think
back on her flimsy answers to every question

about her life   now so obviously a lie   always obviously
a lie that i was too hungry for her sisterhood to notice

distracted by the ways she'd turn the questioning on me
& make me feel interesting   intoxicating me

with her unflinching attention   but now
her words come flooding   fueled by a new anger

rippling beneath the surface   twisting our features
in her face   *we're here because she's going to decide*

what to name the child   *it could have been any name*
but the way the history worked out   *the choices come down*

to nima & yasmeen   *you or me*   *if she chooses yours*
you go back to everything   *& if she chooses mine*

your life becomes mine   & you become like me
& she takes another step toward me   i start to step back

& the wind circles us   carrying with it the smell of the river
the water just below   just behind me

yasmeen, what do you mean like you?   what are you?
& something warps in her face

*the ghost trapped between worlds   the other fading
possibility   that's why you'd go transparent every time*

you wished yourself away   you were making me more real
here i feel a prickle of fear crawl up my neck

*right now you're only half possible   & so am i
whoever's name she chooses   gets to be her daughter*

& she's too close to me now   i look back   nervous
yasmeen, this is really high   can we talk about this downstairs?

& she looks like she is deciding something
a determined look settles onto her face   our face

& she's lunging toward me

pushing me off the roof's concrete   & into open air   & as i fall
i scramble to grab her shirt   pulling her behind me

A Single Possibility

we land   with a hard smack   into the sharp cold
of the river   surrounded by floating trash   submerged
in dirty water   i struggle to keep my head
above the surface   i kick my legs & pull my arms
my body heavy with soaked fabric   yasmeen's grip tight
on a handful of my hair

the waves   which looked so gentle from the shore
splash up into my face   fill my mouth & sting
my burning eyes   they pull me to the surface
as yasmeen submerges me again   desperation
& panic mingling in her face as she forces me back
under the water

& i am so afraid i am almost calm   the thoughts
unspooling slowly before me   i understand her plan
to make herself the only option   eliminate the other
& even when she saved me from that man at the hotel
it wasn't to save me   it was to bring me here
she brought me here to leave me here
to return to my life as herself

she isn't my sister   we are opposite ends of a single
possibility   an only child   forming in
our mother's belly   waiting to be shaped by a name
once & for all   whoever is chosen   lives   & whoever
is not   is gone forever   resolved by history
& so yasmeen   of course   yasmeen is trying to kill me

i scrabble at her hands   now clamped around
my neck   a knot   gnarled & thick   & i feel panic
fluttering the blood away from my fumbling fingers
i claw at her   treading water until i can no longer feel
my legs   i cannot sink   i cannot die & leave my life to her
i cannot leave my loves to her   my mother   haitham
my country frozen in photographs   my tin box of longing
the songs i love   the dance   my cassettes   all mine
not hers   mine

& in a final surge i kick my legs & as i pull myself free
from her grasp   her foot catches on something under
the surface   & she is pulled backward into the depths

Yasmeen

i watch her face disappear under the water   & it is my face
etched with the same panic i feel   coursing through me
& it feels like i am watching myself drown   & i know
i should just let her go   let myself become the only
possibility   eliminate the other

but i can't just leave her there   leave the body
that is my body   to die

& everything feels slowed down   the moment broken
into a string of smaller moments   a tire floats past
& i lunge for it with one hand   my other hand
feeling around   then reaching under the water
for her long braid of hair

i pull   hard   & her head breaches the surface
coughing   arms flailing   grabbing first at me
& then   understanding that i am trying to help
reaching desperately for the tire   *my foot*
she yells hoarsely   *it's caught*   & through
the murk of water i can just make out   the net
snarled around her ankle

& of course the only way to free her   is to suck in a breath
& go underwater   try to keep my eyes open
against the sting   & fumble at the net   worked into
a knot with no give   & through it all   trust that she will not
try again to push me under

right as my lungs are ready to release their scream for air
i work the knot loose   & the net falls away
into the dark depth of the water   i come back up
& gasp hungry breaths   each gulp of air dragging
sharp nails along my throat

yasmeen grabs my hand & helps me throw my arms
over the tire   & together we kick our way back to shore

Yesterday & Tomorrow

we stumble along the riverbank
yasmeen limping beside me

i turn to her & fill with unexpected pity
at the sight of her struggling forward

shrunken by fear & somehow smaller than me
& somehow no longer a threat

no longer some ominous spirit
no longer any better than me   any taller

her breath is ragged & i stop to let her rest
before we walk back along the road

vaguely pointed toward our parents' house
everything a little quieter in the approaching dusk

our dripping hair & clothes making us shiver
in the cooling air

i sneak glances at yasmeen   hunched & unsure
silent in the awkward aftermath of our struggle

& i feel a surge of resentment
i curse my stupid sense of responsibility

to this spirit-girl who still probably wants me dead
who probably would not have saved me

if our places in the water
had been switched

who pushed me into it in the first place

she is quiet   biting her lip
& seems to be squirming inside her skin

as i watch her   before the anger dawns on her face
to match mine   *you don't know what it's like for me*

living nowhere   existing nowhere
stuck watching between worlds

watching you waste all the life you've been given
all that love you've been given

you have no idea what you have
& have the nerve to wish it all away

to wish yourself away   you're the one
that summoned me, stupid

all this talk of wishing you'd been born me
instead of yourself   you called me over

invited me to take the life & make it mine
since you clearly have no use for it

moaning & stuck obsessing over the past
some man that never wanted us to begin with

since you love yesterday so much
why not just stay here

watching history happen like some dumb movie
that doesn't need your participation

& let me do the work of actually living
of actually filling that life you've barely touched

she's right & i hate her for it
& the shame prickles at my warmed skin

as i think back to each time i wished myself gone
wished myself another life

leaving my mother & haitham
behind in the old one

twilight settles around us   the darkening sky
simultaneously brilliant & deep

the moon a perfect orb suspended in the nameless color
& for a moment i look up in wonder

wishing yasmeen would leave me alone
to see the country that was kept from me

go away   i hiss at her   & she rolls her eyes
i wish i could   but in case you haven't noticed, stupid,

i have to go wherever you do
our fates are bound until we figure this out

i promise i'm not hanging around because i like you
& the frustration builds

until i want to tear out my own hair
stop calling me stupid

Dusk

the sun has finished setting as we approach
the gate to the house   to find my mother slipping out
alone   & hurrying down the twilit street
sandals slapping against her heels

yasmeen & i jog to catch up to her   just as the gate
to hala's house opens to let her in   & we're barely inside
before the gate clangs shut
& hala is leading us around the side of the darkened house

we turn in to a back courtyard & the darkness is forgotten
in a cluster of chairs arranged under a string of lanterns
a buzz of laughter & talk & clinking glasses of mint tea

as aisha is whispering   *you didn't have to host tonight*
with everything that's happened   hala cuts her off
i already promised   & it was too late to cancel   it's fine

my mother   holding court with her friends
laughing & teasing & talking more than i've ever heard her
i understand why people want to leave   but i couldn't live

anywhere else   away from everything   i love it here
& i know things can get better   but who will fix it
if we all leave?

khaltu hala laughs & calls her a nationalist   & my mother
not yet my mother   just aisha   throws her head back
to join the laughter

then points up into the night sky   *why go anywhere else*
when we have all the stars   & another friend calls out
here comes the romance   aisha's face is dreamy as she curls

both feet up into the chair   sandals forgotten in the dust
imagine growing up here in our parents' time   she muses
when the country was just born   the elegant way our mothers
would dress

all the independence songs & all that promise   hala pulls
the cigarette from her mouth & laughs again
my nostalgia monster   here i miss haitham with a pang
i don't mean to interrupt the poem

but it's time to put some music on   & a song
rings out into the night   & aisha unfolds
her legs to dance

The Lesson

the song begins crackling through the speakers
يا حبيبي أنا عيان
& i love this one   i sing it to myself & watch
aisha & amal & all the women i'll never know
swaying & clapping & tossing their hair around
to the song   & when it's done something percussive
& powerful takes its place   one of the traditional
dances i love   & as my mother steps into
the center of the circle   i feel myself rising
to echo her   she strikes her foot against
the dust   & i mirror her movements   i bring
my hands to my face in the coy motion she taught me
& swing my hair from side to side   i watch her
in her element   & feel myself in mine   something
in me clicks & stays put & i feel suddenly fluent
in my body   in the knowledge that my waist will move
as i tell it to   that my back will arch in the exact shapes
of hers   & as i twist my head in time to the song's
final notes   i catch yasmeen sitting up   alert
watching me in awe   *how do you do that?*
i keep moving as i answer   *what do you mean?*
i don't know, i don't know what to call it   it's like
you were the music   like your body was the song
how do you do that?

& it begins to dawn on me   slowly at first
then all at once   *yasmeen, have you never*
danced?   & she cuts her eyes at me
don't talk to me like you're sorry for me

165

in case you weren't following what i've been trying
to tell you   i haven't exactly had a body
before this stupid little adventure   so no
i guess i've never danced *before   & wait*
no what are you doing   & i am pulling her up
to join me   her protests slowing as i arrange
her limbs   as i turn to face her   *okay, first*
with your right   & at first her movements
are jerky   uncomfortable   but by the fourth song
her eyes are closed & the music has settled itself
into her muscles   & the movements have begun
to take   mirroring mine   & a few feet away
my mother puts her body through the exact motions
the three of us in parallel

An Alternate Possibility

we sit in a new silence   shy in the aftermath
of our brittle sisterhood   watching the ebb & flow
of the party   & eventually i've had my fill
even the thrill of the old songs i love   not enough
to silence my racing head

i turn to yasmeen   sprawled out in the dust beside me
catching her breath   i nudge her with my foot & she scowls
sits up   ready for another fight   until i raise
my hands in surrender

i just wanted to ask you something   i protest
& she flops back onto the ground   & in her silence i press on
i don't really understand your whole thing   *are you a jinni
or, like, some kind of spirit or something?*

*where were you before i started, i guess, summoning you?
were you trying to steal some other life?*   she doesn't answer
& instead shoots back a question of her own

why did *you summon me? you have this whole big beautiful life
& you're just wasting it, wishing yourself out of it.
how could you not want it?*   & i cast about for the words
to explain   *it's not that i don't want the life*

*i love my mom & haitham & khaltu hala & mama fatheya
& there's a lot of stuff that makes me happy a lot of the time*

it's me i wish were different   i love them & i guess part
of loving them is wishing i were better, a better

version of myself   which i always imagined as you
but i guess you're not actually you? i still need
you to explain it to me. did i, like, invent you?
moments pass & she does not speak   i lean forward
to ask again & she begins

i already told you   i am an alternate possibility
trying to become a person   i don't even know how
to explain it to you   it's like i'm asleep for years at a time
until a living possibility starts to fade

& i see an opening   the memory fades before i wake back up
i basically don't exist without some sort of animating mission
without the pursuit of being born   that's all i want, you know
to be born

it's not even your life i want   i just want a life   any life
i want a person to become   to wake me up for good
i want a body that is mine   actually mine
a body i feel fluent in

do you actually understand how boring it is
waiting to be made possible?

A Life

yasmeen continues   *all this stuff you love   the music,*
the dancing, your mom, haitham   i don't have any of it

i don't have anything like it   & it's all i want

i want a favorite song & i want to know if a guava tastes
the way it looks   i want to shine with sweat

& change colors in the sun   i want to watch television

& memorize whole stretches of movie dialogue   like you
& haitham do   i want the feeling of sitting in hot water

& to be afraid of heights or dogs or the dark

i want to ride the bus   & give someone directions
i want to shell pistachios   & bite my nails   & get the hiccups

from laughing too hard   i want to shield my eyes from the sun
i want eyes that are mine to shield   & skin that is mine

i want goose bumps   & armpits that go damp & i want arms
that are too hairy   or feet that are too large

or anything   i'll take anything   any version of a life

& with a gasp she sits up   my features blurring out
of her face   *i don't think i was supposed to tell you*
any of that

169

Yasmeen

her features flicker in & out   like her whole body
is shimmering with static   hair switching from color
to color   different noses & eyes & mouths arranging
themselves for a moment   before blurring out again

she shakes her head   hard   & the face settles for a moment
one gray eye & one brown   mouth full of large
horsey teeth   *this is bad*   she whispers
a new nose shimmering in to replace the last one

Yasmeen

she begins stumbling around the party   her every
warping feature pleading wordlessly to me for help

i scramble to my feet & hurry toward her   just as
she crashes into a small table   holding half-drunk glasses
of hibiscus juice

before careening toward another table   holding
the cassette player   & i watch in horror as she trips
over the cord   knocking the source

of all the party's music to the ground   & in the new silence
the guests have stopped dancing   watching

as something they cannot see destroys the party around them
yasmeen's face is shining with tears   as the body continues

to knock itself against a tree   like it is trying to rid
itself of her   & before i can reach her   mama fatheya
emerges from the house

a clay incense burner in her hand   billowing dense coils
of smoke   reciting something i don't understand

i watch in horror as the smoke wraps itself around yasmeen
her scream an otherworldly sound   & when the smoke
clears she is gone

Spirits

mama fatheya lifts an upended chair back into its place
& heaves herself into it   as the younger women clamor
around her   she waves away the proffered glass of water

no reason to worry, no reason to be afraid   you all should know
what happens when you play loud music at twilight
when the veil between the spirit world & ours is thinnest
you'll call them to our side   some of them are harmless
but i think this one was particularly nasty

& something in me bristles at hearing
yasmeen described like that   like some sort of monster
hearing someone who doesn't even know her just decide
what she is   what she's like   & with a jolt of panic
i realize i don't know where she's gone   if she's ever
coming back   she isn't evil   she didn't choose
to be this way

i am haunted by the memory of her scream   the sound
of someone in terrible pain   a pain she didn't deserve
when all she ever tried to do was live

Alone

in a corner of the garden i sink
into the soft dirt   my back against the trunk
of a tree wafting gentle notes of jasmine
my heart's painful percussion showing no signs
at first of slowing   until it finally does
& i am left in silence with yasmeen's absence

i thought i'd be relieved   i no longer
have to fight for my name   but i'm still here
with no idea how to leave   how to go home
i'm left with no one else to talk to   no one
who can see me   & she was taken so quickly

i've lost her   & the loss takes its place
among my other losses   & breaks my heart
in new ways   i could have helped her
i've always been the one with everything
i've always been the one with something to give

Alone

time passes & the ruined party continues to disperse
a few stray guests help rearrange the fallen furniture

& gingerly gather the scattered shards of glass
i don't know where to go   i don't know what comes next

& the weariness i've staved off for what feels like days
finally soaks into my body   i want to go home

to my mother   my life   my world where there is room
for me   my world where i have a name   where i am not alone

& in the midst of this thought something is pulling me
to my feet   hands that feel solid as my own

but as i look around wildly
i see no one there

Yasmeen

nima, it's me   & the voice is yasmeen's   *we don't have
a lot of time but i'm here to help*   *i don't have much longer*

but i want to get you home   & i hear the tears in her voice
i tighten my hold on the hand in mine   *yasmeen, wait*

there has to be some way   & she cuts me off   *i don't want it
anymore*   *your life*   *i don't want to take it from you*   *it's yours*

& i can't help but feel stupid for talking tearfully into thin air
but i continue   *yasmeen, there has to be some way i can help*

& her voice takes on a stubborn knot   i can almost picture
the way she shakes her head   the new expressions

she would make of our familiar features   *nima, listen to me.
i don't know why i'm like this. i don't know what it all means.*

*i don't know how to change anything & i don't know anything that
matters*   *except that i can help you get home.*

*i've never wanted to do anything good before, really,
but you're good & you're kind & you're so full of love*

my face gets hot as she says this   *shut up & let me finish,
i mean it*   *even after i literally tried to kill you, you didn't*

think twice about saving me   *you learned this huge thing about
your dad & instead of knocking a hookah over onto his stupid lap,*

your first thought was about helping your mother
& i don't know, it taught me something   so anyway

could you just shut up for a second & let me do my good thing?
& as she mentions baba & the cafe   the idea slams into me

yasmeen, what if we find you a life you don't have to steal?
she's silent for a second   & i take this as permission

to keep going   & hope it doesn't instead mean
she's gone again   *yasmeen?   i'm here.*

what do you mean a life i don't have to steal?

it might not work but we have to try. but is there a way for you
to be less invisible? i can't concentrate when i keep thinking

you've disappeared   & as she flickers back into my sight
her face is once again my face

but rendered in gray scale   like an old photograph

The Plan

yasmeen stumbles along beside me
blurred again around the edges
her fingers going increasingly transparent
where are we going? & how do you know this
is going to work? & also while we're here could you not
say things like 'a life you don't have to steal'   *like you think*
you're better than me?   i look over warily but she's smiling
playful   & i join her   *i'm not saying i'm better   but look*
you're the one who called me 'full of love'   & i can tell
i've embarrassed her   i steel myself for another fight
until   just in time   the cafe looms again
before us   not yet emptied for the night

The Cafe

we slip inside unseen   & weave between
the tables   yasmeen opens her mouth
to protest & i shush her   striding back
toward the table where my father sits
with his friend   with a pang i look away
from him   planning his departure   & i turn
to yasmeen   *remember what his friend was saying*
before they started planning the big escape?
he & his wife want a child   & the child won't appear
is that enough possibility for you?

the plan dawns solidly on her restored face   reanimating
with its new mission   the man rises from the table
& drains his glass   shrugs into his jacket
& claps my father on the shoulder
before slouching toward the door
i pull yasmeen into a hug   tears pricking in my throat
go with him   go get born   go get a body
& before she can speak
i've pushed her out the door behind him

Yasmeen

i stride   triumphant   back toward
my grandmother's house   glowing with
the victory of   hopefully   saving yasmeen
no longer my sister   never actually
my sister   maybe never to be seen
again   but alive somewhere alongside me
our paths untangled & moving in tranquil parallel
i miss my strange almost-friend   her strange
& supernatural company   but i hope i've saved her
& now i need to find a way   to make my name my own

Leaving

i pass through the gate into the garden
& feel my stomach knotting tightly when
i realize   i never asked yasmeen how
to warn my mother   & before i have
a plan   as if summoned   my mother emerges
my father close behind her   his face
tight & expressionless as she reaches for his hand & says
i missed you today   i hope the cinema will cheer you up
& for lack of a better idea
when she passes me i lean in & hiss into
her ear   *don't trust him   he's going*
to leave you   & step back as she startles
& gazes frantically about   to find   of course
nothing   & she climbs   looking troubled
into the car

Breaking

i watch them argue through the window
her face shining with tears   his knuckles
sharp as he grips the steering wheel

he does not look at her   & as she motions
to her stomach with a plea   he strikes
the dashboard   says something curt
& cutting   & i watch her mouth open
then close   she lowers her head
& the tears pour silently into her lap

The Officers

before she can unlock the door to exit
a white pickup truck   piled high
with young men in fatigues   screeches
to a halt beside my parents' little car

five officers debark & crowd toward
the window on my father's side   one knocks
maliciously on the glass   & leans down
grinning when the window lowers & they all
see the beautiful girl in the passenger seat

who is this woman? they call into the window
& my father   collecting himself   replies
she is my wife   no way, so young   another
officer mocks   *we'd like to ask her a few*
questions   licking his chops like a wolf

my father begins to ease the window back up
until one of the men blocks it with the butt
of his rifle   snarls   *we want to ask her*
some questions   then   give us the girl & you
can leave   & it all goes still & silent
as i remember my mother's story   *they shot him*
& i lift a large rock from the others strewn on the road
& aim it hard into the knot of men   they scatter
& peer into the dark   the car has not moved so i heave
another rock & narrowly miss an officer's face

they draw their guns & begin to shoot   i seize up in fear
until i see every bullet passing through me like air
& lodging into tree trunks   parked cars   clanging
into the tin gates of houses   & in the clamor my father
slams his foot   down on the car's accelerator & speeds off
the rifle stuck & rattling against the window   its officer
jogging along with it   until he loses his footing
& falls into the street   & my father does not die

Leaving

when the road is emptied & quiet   the car
inches slowly back toward the house   my father
helping my shaking mother through the gate & into
the courtyard   where they cling to each other
in a long embrace   until her sobs have quieted

stay   she pleads   *or let me come with you*
what happened to us? we love each other
you love me   stay   & he will not look at her
instead   just shakes his head   & leaves her
frozen in the courtyard   as he strides into the house

Gone

i stand   rooted with my mother in the courtyard
as she is racked by new tears   & i also

can't believe that he's gone   i thought i'd helped
i thought i'd fixed it   our broken history full

of loss   full of people & places   once loved
& now simply gone   i thought i'd stolen one back

to our side   reclaimed one of our losses
from history's sharper teeth   from time's gaping mouth

but i was wrong   he was never meant to be ours   my father
he was always meant to be gone   it was always bigger

than anything my small tampering could change
& my mother & i   were always meant to belong

to no one   but each other

Left Behind

my mother is crumpled in her bed   the pillow
on my father's side   undisturbed & smooth
his few clothes & books & records tossed into
the little car   & gone   no one to rub her back
& wipe her face as she convulsed all night with grief

hours pass & the afternoon fills the room with slants
of yellow light   a small knock goes unanswered
then another   & finally khaltu hala slips quietly
into the room   sits sad & quiet at the edge of the bed
considering the hurt radiating from my mother's curled form

they stay in silence for a long moment   hala
places a palm on my mother's searing forehead   & tears
start pouring down the sides of my mother's upturned face
pooling in her ears   down her neck

by sunset khaltu hala convinces her to sit up
& sip water   feeds her pieces of cut fruit   & listens
humming in sympathy as my mother tells her tale
& by the end her face is creased with worry as my mother
says   quietly   *i can't raise his child alone*   *all she*
will do is remind me of him   *i have to give her away*
& my stomach aches into a knot   & i wonder
if i've made everything worse

twilight darkens the room & hala rises to leave
mama is sending me away   *to america*

i have to go home to pack   *& listen*   my mother
raises her eyes to hala without speaking   *aisha, come with me*
i won't leave you here alone   *& i'll be so alone without you*
let's go & start over   *away from everything that hurt us*

The Baby

when hala is gone i take her seat at my mother's bedside
& pass hands she cannot see across her face
over her hair

she stiffens   looks wildly around the room   cries out
in the wrong direction   *who is that? who's there?*

it feels wrong to scare her but i need to change her mind
mama   i plead   *it's me   your daughter   it's me*

& i call to her my name   *i'm your daughter
i need you   we have a whole life together   together*

you're all i need   not him   you're all i need   please
& my mother slows her frantic search around the room

& looks   awed   down at her stomach   touches it
reverently   & in the quiet wraps her voice around
my name

nima   repeats it like a prayer   *nima   nima
my saving grace*   & as she says my name a chasm

opens where once lay my father's abandoned pillow
colors swirling as if in water   before settling

into a scene   i peer into the opening & see the bathroom
of our apartment   water running into the tub   about

to overflow   i look back at my mother   hurt but surviving
cradling her belly   crooning my name to herself   *nima*

PART 3

HOME IS NOT
A COUNTRY

The Portal

the gap in this world is pulling me toward it
like a current   inside it the bathtub has begun
to overflow   glistening onto the tile
& i don't know if i'm ready to leave   i have
so much left to do   to see   i have to study
my grandmother's long-lost face   learn the lives
of all those i didn't know before their great losses
the men in the band   i want to know what happens
to haitham's father   if he is ever seen again
i want to know why they all left   & undo all the damage
undo the wars   the hunger   the kidnapped women
& jailed men   returning months later looking hollowed out
hair shorn close against their skulls   i want to fix it all
i want to help   in this world where i don't feel so helpless
so hunted   where i don't have to watch haitham's
broken face without knowing if he's still alive
behind it   where my arabic flows easily
from my throat   & the athan rings out five times
a day from the minarets   in a voice husky with magic
i want to eat guava & skip stones into the stinking river
i want to watch my mother's youth   her dancer's
walk   her life vibrant with friendship & parties
styled like a film star in her yellow dress   not tired
not at work   & instead laughing   dancing
clapping along to all the songs she loves   her unbroken
country   pulled warm around her   & i fight hard
against the portal's pull   i reach to grip a bedpost
& my hands move clean through it like it's water

i grab at everything around me as it dissolves back
to history   my feet now submerged to the ankle
in the chasm   i make one final
reach for my mother's frozen arm   & it blurs away
the portal moving up my legs to swallow me whole

The Portal

the portal is uncomfortably hot   pulls me by its current
toward the other side   & all around me
swirling like autumn leaves   are hundreds
of photographs i've never seen
arriving to paper the walls of the tunnel

in one   my mother pregnant at the airport
smiling hugely into her new life   in another
my mother cradles a tiny baby in awe
one taken the winter when i first befriended haitham
when my mother bought me a new coat   & shivered
every day in her layers of sweaters   my mother
folding me tiny paper boats to float in the bathtub
my mother demonstrating a movement to a group of girls
twisting to mirror it   my mother smiling broadly
beneath a sign that reads   *traditional dance classes by aisha*
my mother in a newspaper clipping whose caption reads
founder of local dance troupe banat al-nima describes dance
as her connection to a lost home   & in every photo
my hand is clutched tight in hers   or around her leg
or tugging on her hem   in every photo we are together

not a single one   where either one of us is alone   & in a rush
of warm air the portal deposits me   feetfirst & fully clothed
into the bathtub   splashing water over the sides
my mother knocking frantically outside the bathroom door

Home

i call to her & i hear her voice weighted with relief   a sob
catching in her throat   *you're here   you're here*
i thought i'd lost you   where have you been all day?
& i heave myself out of the tub to unlock the door
dripping a trail of bathwater behind me

my mother pulls me to her   my wet clothes soaking hers
her tears spilling into my hair   & the words pour out
in both languages from my mouth   *i'm sorry   i'm sorry*
you're all the family i need   you're all the parent i need
i'm sorry   thank you for making us this life from nothing
thank you for choosing me   i'm sorry   i choose you too
i choose you   you're all i need   you're all of it
& we stand like this   clasped & sobbing
until i start to shiver in my still-drenched clothes
she wraps me in a towel   sends me
to my room to change

The Photographs

& in the apartment outside all but one of the photographs

of my father have disappeared   replaced instead by the ones

from the portal   the one with me as a newborn

framed in the living room

the one at the airport   taped to the mirror

of my mother's dresser

in the one on the coffee table we perch

by a bathtub crowded with paper boats

& in the absence of his face i finally pay attention

to the others   all over the apartment

that have been there all along

my grandmother   my mother surrounded

by friends & smiling enormously into the camera

my mother grinning beside khaltu hala

my mother holding a bouquet of flowers

surrounded by girls in dancers' clothes

what is newest is a poster   advertising

the banat al-nima dance school   & on it a photograph

of my mother midstep   & across from her

in the exact movement   is me

& when i pull my tin box from beneath the bed

the one photograph remains   my parents at the party

& with it is a new one of my mother   here in america

in full color at some recent party   yellow dress

swirling bright around her   head thrown back

her mouth open midlaugh or midlyric

arms stretched above her head

as if in victory   aisha   bright & full of living

The Kitchen

i change into dry clothes & emerge from my room
to see my mother in the kitchen cutting fruit   a pot
of lentils rioting on the stove   i watch her quietly
drinking her in   she looks younger   less tired
less stooped around the shoulders   undefeated

she turns her head & catches me looking   smiles
holds up some tupperware & nods toward the pot
of food   *i thought we'd take this to the hospital*
& have dinner with haitham's family   & the world i left
behind begins steadily to fade   as i rejoin mine
& in my world haitham is in the hospital   his body broken
struggling to stay alive   & i fight the urge to dissolve
into tears   into hopelessness over the fact
that i've changed nothing that matters   i clench my jaw
to keep back the sobs   & join mama in the kitchen
to scrape the burnt bits of rice at the bottom of the pot
haitham's favorite   into a separate container
for when he wakes up   i reply to her glance

Haitham

when i met you we were so small   so miraculously
unhurt   unawoken by the dreams that make our mothers
scream out at night   the whole world our private joke
the whole world a playground for our twinned brains
your perfect heart   its daily forgiveness of my uglier one

when i met you i had a father   or at least i had the dream
of one   to lull me every night to sleep
photos to study   to imagine   separated only
by the spirit world's veil   a father who would
choose me   & would have   if he could have   stayed
but now i have so much more   i have so much to tell you
wake up   i have so much left to say

when i met you we were such children   believing neither
of us could ever die   won't you wake up   wake up
& believe it with me again

Haitham

i approach haitham's bedside   my mother busying herself
unpacking the dishes   his mother & grandmother each
in her own gnarled sleep in a chair

i don't know if i'm allowed to touch him   if it will hurt him
they've taken the tube from his mouth   & his lip
has healed a little   though his eyes stay closed
& solemn   & i can't tell if he's breathing   i lean in
to listen for a heartbeat   for a breath
& his voice bubbles out   unchanged
excuse me, a little personal space   & i feel
like my heart just shot up to my throat
i straighten to look at him & his eyes
are wide open   wide awake   his grin
threatening to split his lip back open   i squeal
& laugh & burst into tears

i'm sorry   i wail   & he cocks an eyebrow
winces a little & straightens his face   *sorry for what?*
& when i reach for the memory of our argument   it's like
trying to remember a dream   like trying to carry water
in a cupped palm   all of it trickling slowly away   *i . . .*
you . . .   *i . . .*   *i can't really remember*
i blurt out   sheepish   he looks at me
mock-serious   *did you also get kicked in the head?*
then laughs his enormous laugh

Haitham

when i met you i was already angry   so angry
about everything i thought had been taken from me
everything i thought i did not have   so busy looking
at my one empty hand   i almost missed everything
filling the other

i think i spent a long time hating myself   thinking
of myself as not enough   thinking i was loving
everyone i loved by wishing a better version of myself
into their lives   one more deserving   more graceful

i think i could have been a better friend to you
instead of locking myself away inside my head
& invented memories   locking myself away
inside the old photographs   the old songs
& letting my whole life happen without me

is what i want to say but all i can manage is
i'm here now & i want to do better
& i'm sorry & i missed you & thank you,
thank you for waking up   & haitham looks
for a moment like he is about to make a joke
& then   miraculously   doesn't
instead says   simply   *nima, you're my best friend*
but of course   can't help himself   *but didn't*
the doctor tell you not to make me cry
& i am already smothering him in a hug
pressing tighter & marveling at him   so solid
& alive   until i hear his muffled *ouch*

Home Is Not a Country

i've returned to my life   only to find that things
aren't all that different   i go to school & wave
at haitham in the hallways & eat my lunch alone
in the company of others eating their lunches alone
though this morning while i make yet another
tragic sandwich   my mother appears   her face
determined   & sets something neatly wrapped
in paper towels on the counter before me

nima, please, enough with those awful sandwiches
will you take this instead?   *it's cheese like i know*
you like, but it's feta & i heated some pita & there's
fuul & tomato in there too   *i can't keep imagining*
my daughter at school eating that plastic   here she
casts a grim look at the neon slices of cheese
in their individual sleeves   & i feel a dread
i hadn't realized i was carrying   dissolve as i imagine
myself eating a lunch that doesn't make me want
to cry

The Singer

at the bigala my mother haggles with the shopkeeper
seriously? for just the one leg of lamb? can you prove

to me it descended from isaac?   while i browse
along the shelf of tapes   selecting two & bringing them

to the counter   the shopkeeper barely glancing at me
before turning   probably to shout back at my mother

but does a double take   he lifts one of the cassettes
to the light   *oh, i love this one*   & sings dreamily

to himself   in a voice like honey   يا حبيبي أنا عيان
& i recognize   behind the scowling face i've always known

that singer from the party   the looseness of his limbs
his freedom   but it already feels like something from

a dream   or an old film i watched once then lost to time
but still i say   *you have a beautiful voice, uncle*

& my mother twinkles up at him   *you didn't know?*
back home he was something of a celebrity

& the laugh softens his grizzled face   as he wraps the lamb
up for my mother & hands it to her   *consider it a gift*

for the dancer & her daughter

Nima

& now on saturdays my mother teaches her class
rows of girls in all our people's sepia shades

arranged eagerly before her in our living room
the furniture pushed back into the corners

as they learn all the shapes & the songs
& the particular language of the drum

i love to watch her teach   & love it more when she calls
me out of my room   to demonstrate one thing

or another   *watch nima*   she'll say
& i'll feel the eyes warming my skin

as i reach for the song & wrap it tightly around me
& my body responds in its language

Yasmeen

we're back in arabic class   haitham's stitches healed over
& his cast covered in scribbled signatures
stickers & cartoons   & though it's his left
when the teacher brings over a quiz

& tries to hand haitham the sheet   he lifts his cast
& announces   *this is my writing hand, sir*
& is excused from all work until it heals

when the teacher turns i shove him in his
good shoulder   *liar*   *you're never going to learn
any arabic*   & he looks over   face contorted
in pretend heartbreak   *my arabic is perfect*   *listen*
نار يا حبيبي نار   we collapse into laughter
before he finishes the lyric

& hear a third voice laughing with us   a girl   sitting
behind haitham   leans forward over her desk
her round face is full of mischief   eyes big & dark
& already in on the joke

her lips stretch into a smile   full of large
white teeth   gilded in multicolored braces
she smells faintly of sesame & flowers
something about her distantly familiar
though i can't place it

& as if to answer the question i haven't yet asked
she holds out her hand   acting out a serious

handshake   *hi, i'm new, my name's jazzy*
& haitham raises an eyebrow

that's not arabic, is it?   come on, what's
your passport name?   & she makes a face
everyone calls me jazzy   or jazz
except my mom when she's mad   then
she calls me yasmeen

Jazz

sits between me & mama fatheya on the couch
both of them engrossed in the same cooking show
while haitham sits by our feet   trying & failing
to work a series of objects under his cast
to scratch his arm   during commercials
jazzy rouses mama fatheya with her perfect arabic
& just as i feel a strange & ancient jealousy
unfurling in my chest
she turns to me & grins   *i hear you're some kind*
of nostalgia monster   so i come bearing an offering
& from the pocket of her jacket she extracts
an unlabeled tape
did you know our arabic teacher was in a band back home
with a bunch of the uncles from the building?   & would you
believe they were actually good? there's an amazing cover
of this sayed khalifa song on here that i love
& we are instantly kindred   she unfolds
her long legs from the couch & reaches
for my hand   & as i grab it i feel a familiar
pressure in her grasp
that familiar scent   floral & earthy
& echoing with something
i know i've known but have forgotten
& i blurt out   *not to be weird   but i feel*
like i know you from somewhere
haitham looks up from attending to his arm
& calls out   *all these love songs are making you such*
a romantic   to which yasmeen   laughing   replies
shut up   can't you see we're having a moment, stupid?

& for a second   her voice wrapped around the word
is almost a memory   almost a song from another life
& when i reach for it   it is gone
as the old cassette player
crackles out the song   وين الحلوين وين راحوا
where are the beautiful ones   where did they go

Yellow

my dreams are vivid   a world of blue & sepia
the smells of guava & smoke   car exhaust & charred peanuts
a city built around two rivers   the site of their joining
faces vaguely familiar   brown skin shining with sweat
with perfumed oil   a song that never stops playing
thick gnarl of a doum tree   bright shock of bougainvillea
eloquent stink of that faraway river

& then i wake up   pale sunlight streaming in
& the room lights up around me   photographs taped
to the wall above my bed   cassettes & cds shelved messily
in the far corner   an arabic workbook splayed
on the floor   filled with earnest cursive scrawls

i sit up & blink away the last of the dream
its colors retreating   outside the day is unseasonably
warm   i float sleepily into the morning
brushing my teeth   splashing water
onto my pillow-creased face   the kitchen wafting warm
& milky smells   & back in my room   spread
like a ray of sunlight across the unmade bed
is mama's yellow dress   calling to me almost
by name   i rush toward it with a squeal
of excitement   hurry out of my pajamas & slip it over
my head   & the silk shimmers around me
like something liquid

i turn to the mirror & twirl   like the girl in the photograph
like aisha before me   & midspin i catch her standing

in the doorway   the beautiful girl who became my mother
her face buoyant & alive as she claps her hands   *oh, nima*
you were made for that color   & i feel warm in the yellow
in my belonging to her as she names me   *my precious girl*
my graceful one

ACKNOWLEDGMENTS

Even during the times when I did not know where I was from, I have always known those to whom I belong. My communities are my country, are my home, are my place in the world. This book is for them, and made possible by them, by the ways their love has held and shaped me.

Before this book, I might have been happy to spend the rest of my life only doing the things I already knew how to do. I am grateful to Christopher Myers for the invitation to grow, for meeting me for breakfast whenever I needed to remember that the tools I already had could be used in new ways. Thank you for your friendship, and for your faith in me. Thank you to Ammi-Joan Paquette, my agent, for the phone calls, for being the first reader of the manuscript that would become this book, for taking a chance on me. Thank you to Michelle Frey, my editor, for your care, for the warmth and rigor of your eye, for sculpting this book with me.

Every word I write is in gratitude to my many teachers, to the lateral mentorship I found among my peers, who are so unselfish with what they know, who teach me with poems and group chats and emails and long impromptu phone calls. Thank you to Elizabeth Acevedo, this book's auntie; I am grateful for your sisterhood, your generosity, and for the better worlds you've dreamt for us. Thank you to Clint Smith, to Team Cowork. Thank you to Team Mashallah, my siblings: Fatimah Asghar, Angel Nafis, Hanif Abdurraqib, Kaveh Akbar. Thank you to my Beotis family, to my Stegner cohort, and to the communities I've found at Cave Canem, Slam! at NYU, the DC Youth Slam Team, and Split This Rock. To Kamau Brathwaite, Louise Glück, Eavan Boland, Patrick Phillips, and Mark Bibbins—I am grateful for your classrooms and your considerate attention, under which I've watched myself blossom into newer and more infinite shapes.

To my childhood besties, my Scorpios, my long unbroken line: Basma Rustom and Awrad Saleh. Gonna love you forever, like I've been doing.

The greatest and most important honor of my life is being the daughter of Safaa El-Kogali, the sister of Almustafa Elhillo, the granddaughter of Habab Elmahdi and Eltayeb El-Kogali, a niece and a cousin to my huge and rowdy and incredible family. Thank you to my ancestors for all my names, for the stories. I hope you'll never stop telling them to me.

Christopher Gabriel Núñez, my love, my lifelong accomplice. Thank you for building this life with me. Thank you for the hours spent answering and re-answering all my questions about narrative, for that syllabus you made me, for being my partner in every sense, for your enormous laugh and for making breakfast. This book is one of the thousand ways you are generous. Thank you for the gift of your family. Thank you to Margarita and Fernando, to Karina and Tatiana and JP, to tías Olga and Fanny.

To the global Sudanese community, particularly in the DMV and New York and the Bay Area: thank you for this immense siblinghood, for teaching me that a home is a thing to be made, not to be lost or found. Thank you for reminding me of the fact of my own hands. Thank you for being the funniest people on the planet, and for knowing exactly how to make me cry. I am proud to be yours and to know that my name lives among your names.